ANDREA CARTER AND THE

Long Ride Home

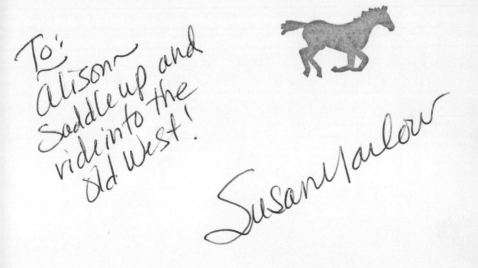

To:
Alison—
Saddle up and
ride into the
Old West!

Susan Marlow

ANDREA CARTER AND THE

Long Ride Home

Susan K. Marlow

Kregel
Publications

Andrea Carter and the Long Ride Home

© 2005 by Susan K. Marlow

Published by Kregel Publications, a division of Kregel, Inc., P.O. Box 2607, Grand Rapids, MI 49501.

Library of Congress Cataloging-in-Publication Data
Marlow, Susan K.
Andrea Carter and the long ride home: a novel / by Susan K. Marlow.
        p. cm. (Circle C adventures)
    1. Ranch life—California—Fiction. 2. Runaways—Fiction.
3. Horses—Fiction. 4. Christian life—Fiction. 5.
California—History—1850–1950—Fiction. I. Title.
PZ7.M34528And   2005
[Fic]—dc22   2005006620

ISBN 0-8254-3188-3

Printed in the United States of America

05 06 07 08 09 / 5 4 3 2 1

For Lisa Otto,
who *insisted* this story should be published
and
for my sons, Andrew and Ryan,
who always begged me to read
"just one more chapter."

Chapter One

IT'S NOT FAIR!

I t's Saturday at last!" Andi Carter leaped from her bed and threw open the doors that led onto the balcony of her family's two-story ranch house. She hurried out into the early morning, leaned far over the railing, and breathed in the fresh new California day. "This is going to be a great day," she announced in delight, tossing her unruly mass of long, dark curls behind her shoulder. She could not hide her joy at the thought of a whole day to ride her horse, Taffy, and do as she liked.

She leaned farther over the railing, hoping to catch a glimpse of her brother Chad's new stallion. The corral next to the barn was just beyond sight, but if she climbed over the railing and balanced on the narrow overhang, she might be able to see the magnificent animal— if only for a moment. Putting thoughts into action, she scurried over the top, hampered only slightly by her long, white nightgown. She could almost hear her mother's disapproving voice. *"Really, Andrea. Proper young ladies do* not *climb balconies in their nightgowns!"* She smiled at the thought and shaded her eyes against the rising sun.

Before she could get a good view of the horse, the sun cleared the distant peaks of the Sierra Nevada, and she was forced to narrow her eyes against the brightness that erupted around her. The ranch house, styled after the lovely and practical Spanish *haciendas* of an earlier age, burst into dazzling white against the bright blue sky.

"I can't see a thing," she muttered, disappointed.

"*Buenos días, señorita,*" a cheerful voice hailed her from below. "What are you doing?"

Andi whirled around, slipped, and nearly lost her balance. She reached out to steady herself against the railing, and looked down. Diego, one of the hired hands, stood leaning against a rake, grinning up at her.

"I . . . well . . . I was trying to see Chad's new stallion," came her embarrassed reply. She hastily climbed back over the railing and onto the safety of the balcony.

Diego glanced in the direction of the corral, then up at the girl. He shook his head. "Why do you not go and look at the horse from nearer the corral, like everyone else?"

Andi felt herself turning red and said nothing. Instead, she spun around and re-entered her bedroom, closing the doors with a bang. "What a way to start the day," she mumbled. But she couldn't help breaking into a grin at how she must have looked, hanging onto the balcony and wearing only her nightgown. No doubt Diego was having a good laugh over it while he tended the gardens.

She hurried across her room and began to dress, pulling on her favorite pair of faded overalls and a gingham shirt. How glad she was that her mother didn't always force her to wear what other young ladies going on twelve had to wear—dresses and tiny slippers and other uncomfortable trappings. On Saturdays, she was allowed to wear what she pleased, so long as she didn't step foot off the ranch.

"After all," Andi declared, pulling on one of her riding boots, "this *is* 1880. There are a lot of new ideas about what a girl can wear."

A door slammed loudly. Andi paused in her dressing and listened. Only Chad slammed doors like that, and then only when he was upset about something.

"Andi! Get down here!" Chad's voice traveled up the stairs and through her bedroom door like the sound of a gunshot.

Andi winced. *Oh great. I wonder what I've done wrong this time.* She quickly pulled on the other boot and made her way to the vanity. Pouring the tiniest amount of water from the milk-white pitcher into the washbasin, she splashed the cold liquid onto her face. A small knot of worry began to form in her stomach as she hastily braided her thick, dark hair into two long plaits. What could have upset Chad first thing in the morning?

She stood up, gave a quick glance around her less-than-spotless room, and frowned. She knew she should take time to straighten it, but if she didn't find out what Chad wanted, he'd start yelling again. "I'll clean it later," she decided, half hoping that Luisa, their house keeper, might look in on her room and spare a few minutes to clean it for her.

She made her way from her room but stopped at the top of the stairs. Reaching out her hand, she ran it along the smooth surface of the banister. *Just this once*, she persuaded herself. Determined not to let Chad ruin her morning, she settled herself onto the railing. Lifting her feet, she sailed down the banister and landed on the foyer floor with a loud *thump*. She grinned as she picked herself up from the floor. Sliding down the banister was such fun!

Her cheerful mood instantly restored, Andi entered the dining room with a spring in her step. She greeted her mother and older sister, who were finishing their breakfast in companionable silence.

"Good morning, Andrea," her mother replied with a smile. "Luisa just brought in a fresh plate of hotcakes. Sit down and have some before they get cold."

Andi sat down in the empty seat next to her sister and pretended not to notice that seventeen-year-old Melinda hadn't returned her greeting. She shrugged it off and helped herself to a stack of still-warm pancakes, smothering them in butter and maple syrup. *She's probably mad at me*, Andi concluded. *Somebody's always mad at me these days.*

"Chad's looking for you," Melinda announced, breaking the silence.

"I know," Andi replied uneasily. "I heard him. The whole ranch can hear him when he yells."

"I wonder what upset him this early in the day," her mother remarked with a frown.

Andi didn't know, but she was certain it wouldn't be long before she found out. Her cheerful mood began to dissolve.

"So, here you are."

Andi looked up. Her twenty-six-year-old brother stood just inside the doorway. It was easy to see he was irritated about something. He wasn't smiling, and his blue eyes were stormy. He lifted a finger and pointed it at Andi. "I'd like a word with you."

"What about?" She speared a forkful of pancake and swirled it around in the syrup. She hoped Chad wasn't in one of his bossy moods. Just because he was in charge of running the ranch, it certainly didn't mean he could tell her what to do all the time. She scowled.

"I've just come from the barn," Chad explained, "where I discovered about a dozen thirsty horses—yours included."

Andi sprang from her chair in sudden panic. Her blue eyes widened at the awful realization she had neglected her chores. "Oh, no!" she burst out. "I'm sorry! I forgot. I'll do it right away." She hurried around the table, but Chad held out his arm to prevent her leaving.

"Never mind. Mitch is taking care of it." He shook his head. "You were supposed to do it yesterday after school."

"I know, but . . ." Her voice faltered. "Some of the men were breaking those new broncos out in the north corral, and they said I could watch for a few minutes. I was going to check the horses after supper, but—" She broke off. "I'm sorry," she finished lamely.

Chad folded his arms across his chest and looked down at his sister. He nodded at her overalls and boots. "I'm glad to see you're dressed for work today. You're going to muck out every stall in the horse barn."

"Muck out the *stalls*?" Andi's voice rose in disbelief. "That's the ranch hands' job, not mine."

"Today it's your job."

"It'll take all day!"

"Good. It'll keep you out of trouble."

"Mother!" Andi turned to her mother in a desperate appeal. "Please don't make me clean stalls today. It's my only free day. I want to go riding."

Elizabeth Carter's soft blue eyes were full of understanding, but her voice was firm. "I'm sorry, Andrea. This is the third time in two weeks Chad's had to remind you about those horses. Checking their water is not a difficult task. Perhaps cleaning out stalls will help your memory."

Andi opened her mouth to protest. She closed it when she realized her mother was not going to budge. Ever since her father's death in an accident during spring round-up six years ago, her mother had turned over the running of the ranch to Andi's three older brothers. She rarely went against any decision Chad made regarding the day-to-day management of the ranch.

"Better get started," Chad suggested. He poured himself a cup of coffee and joined his mother and Melinda at the table.

"It's not fair," Andi grumbled, reaching across the table for some sugar for her horse. "One little mistake." She pocketed the sugar and turned toward the door. "My whole day is ruined."

She left the house and kicked the dust in frustration as she made her way toward the huge barn that stabled some of the finest horses in the San Joaquin Valley. Though most of the working horses were kept outdoors in a large corral, to be lassoed each day for work, there were always a few stabled in the barn. It was Andi's job to feed and water them.

She reached the barn and leaned briefly against the wide double doors before entering. "Oh, Justin, I wish you were home. I'm hardly ever in trouble when you're around." She sighed. Her eldest brother had gone to Sacramento—again. Why couldn't he stay home and help Chad and Mitch run the ranch, instead of rushing off to San Francisco or Sacramento every few months? "I'm sure the governor can run the state of California without your help," she muttered angrily. It was an old story. Justin was often away—doing whatever it was lawyers do—and no amount of wishing would bring him home any sooner.

With a sudden, urgent desire to get the miserable stall-cleaning job done, Andi pushed Justin from her thoughts, shoved the heavy barn doors open, and slipped inside, adjusting her eyes to the dim interior. The familiar odors of dusty hay, horses, and old leather greeted her.

She paused a moment to enjoy the sweet smell of last summer's alfalfa, then picked up a pitchfork, found the wheelbarrow, and made her way to her horse's stall. The palomino mare whinnied with eagerness at the sight of her young mistress. She thrust her golden head over the stall's half-door and nipped playfully at Andi's shoulder. *Let me out of here!* she seemed to be saying.

"I know you hate being cooped up, Taffy. I guess I'm just being selfish. You stay so much cleaner indoors." She unlatched the stall's door and entered, patting the horse in apology. "I'm sorry, but your troubles are nothing compared to mine." She began to clean the stall and unload her complaints onto her best friend, the one companion who always listened patiently. "I can't do *anything* right these days," she complained.

She stopped and leaned on the pitchfork. "Oh, Taffy! How could I have been so *stupid* to leave that open jar of spiders in Melinda's room last week?" She lunged savagely at a pile of soiled bedding and tossed it through the open doorway. The load missed the wheelbarrow and landed in the middle of the walkway. She sighed. "Nobody believed me when I said it was an accident. I only wanted to see the new stallion Chad and Mitch were bringing home. Everybody knows Melinda's room has the best view of the corral. I didn't mean to forget about the spiders. Really, I didn't. Everything just happened so fast when the stallion broke out. Two of the men almost got trampled, and Jake Barnes got his arm broke!"

Andi gave Taffy a shove to encourage her to move over. "You should have seen Melinda at breakfast the next morning. She slammed the empty jar down right in front of me. When I saw those red bites all over her face and arms, I knew I was in trouble. Guess what I did the rest of the morning?" She walked around to face her horse. "Are you listening, Taffy?"

Taffy stamped an impatient foot. Andi took it as a sign that she should continue her tale. "I spent the entire morning searching for and killing spiders. Then Mother made me scrub every crack in Melinda's floor and wash down the walls. I've decided not to collect spiders anymore." She shook her head sadly, remembering her sister's mood at breakfast. "I think Melinda's still mad at me."

Andi leaned the pitchfork against the wall and turned back to her horse, giving the animal an affectionate pat. Taffy snorted and tossed her head, as if eager to hear more.

"If spiders aren't bad enough, listen to what happened in school last week." She grabbed a brush and started grooming the beautiful golden palomino's coat. "Remember that big frog I found near the creek a couple of weeks ago? I took it to school. Cory and I had a deal. He was going to swap me five aggies for the frog. But before we could make the trade at recess, Miss Hall found the frog in my desk." She cringed at the memory. "She scolded me in front of the entire class and sent me to the corner. The corner, Taffy! I was in disgrace the rest of the day." Andi sighed. "Now, I've got no frog and no marbles."

She tossed the brush into a corner and picked up the pitchfork once more. Spiders, frogs, forgetting her chores, leaving her room a mess—the list went on and on. She shook her head sadly. Absolutely nothing had gone right since Justin left for Sacramento, and here she was on her only free day—stuck in the barn.

She heard a sudden, distinctive whinny and returned from another spell of daydreaming. She finished up Taffy's stall and leaned the pitchfork against one of the large posts that supported the loft above. The whinny came again, a call from the corral next to the barn.

Andi peeked through the open barn door and into the corral. A rush of longing filled her heart. There he was: Chad's new black stallion. He was a monstrous horse—well over sixteen hands high—with a temper to match his size. He was the most beautiful horse Andi had ever seen. And the most dangerous.

From the moment the stallion had arrived on the ranch, Andi had begged to help with the gentling. Horses trusted her, she insisted. There wasn't a horse on the entire ranch she couldn't ride.

All her pleading had amounted to nothing. She was allowed to watch Chad work with the stallion—from a safe distance—but told never to go near him alone.

"It's not fair." Andi scowled and watched the magnificent horse run along the corral fence. "If only Chad would give me a chance. I'd show him that horse would like me."

She leaned against the doorpost and shoved her hands into her pockets, ignoring her chores and gazing at the gorgeous black animal. She felt a few small, hard lumps at the bottom of her pocket and remembered Taffy had not yet been given her weekly treat of sugar.

With a sigh, Andi pulled the sugar from her pocket and turned toward Taffy's stall. She paused. A tiny flickering of an idea tickled the back of her mind. She uncurled her fingers and stared at the small, white lumps lying in her palm. Her heart fluttered. *I know I can do it,* she decided suddenly. She raised her head and looked over at the stallion. *I'll show Chad his stallion isn't as wild as he thinks.* She took a step away from the barn and into the yard.

Chapter Two

A CLOSE CALL

A ndi stopped and gave a low whistle, the same greeting Chad always used to announce his presence to the horse. She waited, holding her breath. The stallion stopped short. He pricked up his ears and turned his head in her direction. With that sign of encouragement, Andi relaxed. She made her way slowly and quietly toward the corral, whistling softly.

The stallion shied away to the other side of the corral when Andi approached. He paced nervously back and forth and stamped the ground in confusion. He seemed to recognize the whistle but not the girl. He laid his ears back in warning. Andi hesitated. She glanced cautiously around the yard for any sign of life. It was deserted.

Little by little, she hoisted herself onto the top railing of the corral and sat quietly, watching the animal. The horse regarded her for an instant, and then moved a few paces closer. Was his curiosity getting the better of him?

"C'mon, you beautiful thing," Andi urged in a low whisper. "You know I'd never hurt you, don't you? Listen. I whistle just like Chad." She whistled softly and waited. The horse snorted and shook his head, then advanced a few more steps.

Andi glanced down into her open hand. The lumps of sugar were beginning to melt. She took a deep breath and extended her palm. "See here, horse. I've got you one special treat. I brought it out for Taffy, but if you come over here and show me you can behave, I'll let you have it." Her voice was calm, gentle, and convincing.

The stallion looked interested. He took a few more steps, then whinnied and trotted away. He stopped at the far end of the corral and regarded Andi with wild eyes.

Andi whistled again. She was prepared to stay on top of the fence the rest of the morning—or until someone caught her—to convince that horse to do one thing: eat sugar from her hand. *Chad will surely let me help out when he sees his wild stallion taking sugar from me!* The thought made her smile, and she held out her hand a little farther.

"C'mon, fella," Andi whispered. She continued to whistle and speak softly. The horse pranced and tossed his head, then suddenly rose up on his hind legs.

Andi gasped. The stallion was so magnificent she could scarcely breathe. She could see powerful muscles flexing under the shimmering black coat. He advanced to within a few arm-lengths of her and came down on all fours, snorting his uneasiness and curiosity.

Andi's eyes grew wide at his nearness. She tightened her grip on the fence and bit her lip in sudden indecision. He was so *huge* up close. Taking a few deep breaths to still her pounding heart, she extended her hand as far as she could without tumbling into the corral.

"Come and get it, beauty," she crooned. The horse took a step. "That's right, boy," she encouraged, "One more step and it's yours." She sat perfectly still, silently willing the stallion closer. She wanted nothing more than to touch his velvet nose.

The horse shook his mane and nibbled at the sugar in Andi's outstretched palm. Her heart swelled with joy. "I knew it!" she bursted out. "Just wait 'til Chad—"

Without warning, the enormous animal reared up and screamed a challenge. The blood drained from Andi's face at the sound. Her mind shouted, *Jump down!* But she couldn't move. Her arms and legs were frozen with fear. She choked back a cry and watched in horror as the stallion's huge, black hooves bore down on her.

An instant later, she found herself flying backward through the air.

She landed in the dust with a painful *thud* and heard a tremendous *crack*. The stallion's hooves connected with the corral fence and brought it tumbling down.

Andi lay on the ground a few yards from the corral and tried to catch her breath, which came in huge gasps. She was shaking so badly, she couldn't even sit up. She had no idea how she'd managed to escape. Had the stallion kicked her off the fence? If so, why was she still alive? She glanced around the yard. It was suddenly alive with activity. Ranch hands appeared from nowhere. They scurried around the corral in an attempt to keep the frantic horse contained.

A shadow fell across her, and Andi looked up. Chad towered over her, hands on his hips, glaring. She had never seen him so furious. His face was dark with anger, and his eyes were chips of blue ice. He shouted some instructions at the ranch hands, and then turned all of his attention to the small figure huddled on the ground.

"What were you *doing*?" he bellowed. The whole ranch could hear him. "You could have been killed!"

Andi bit back a yelp of pain when her brother jerked her up from the ground. He led her over to the splintered railings. "Look at this!" he commanded loudly. "That's where you were sitting, not one minute ago. It's ruined. Destroyed. If I hadn't come around the barn and yanked you off that fence when I did, you'd be dead now—trampled by a horse you have no business going near."

Andi swallowed hard and stared at the ruined fence. She heard in Chad's shaking voice not only anger, but fear for her safety. She had scared him badly with her disobedience, and she was ashamed.

"I'm sorry," she finally whispered.

"You're *sorry*!" Chad took a deep breath and removed his hat. He wiped the sweat from his forehead and ran his fingers through his thick, black hair. Then he replaced the hat and slowly shook his head. "What's wrong with you lately? You're supposed to be in the barn doing your chores. Instead, you're out here causing the worst kind of trouble." He took his sister firmly by the shoulders and forced her to look him in the eye. "I told you to stay away from this horse. Have you already forgotten about Jake's arm? Or those other two hands who were nearly trampled?"

Andi shook her head, valiantly holding back her tears at Chad's rebuke. She hadn't forgotten. She had simply taken for granted that the horse wouldn't hurt *her*. How wrong she had been! She took a deep breath and turned her attention toward the now quiet stallion. "I only wanted to show you I could help with—"

"No." Chad held up his hand to cut her off. "I don't want to hear any more excuses. You'd best get back to your chores before I really lose my temper."

"Chad, *please*!" Andi pleaded. "I said I was sorry. Won't you listen?"

"Not this time." Chad glanced over his sister's head to where the men were making repairs on the fence. A shudder went through him. "One more thing, little sister," he said firmly, turning his attention back to Andi. He raised a finger and pointed toward the stallion. "If I *ever* catch you near that horse again, I'll tan your backside."

Andi caught the looks of several ranch hands who had paused to listen. She turned bright red. "You'll have to catch me first!" she challenged. Her embarrassment gave way to sudden fury. How dare he say that in front of the hired hands! "*I hate you!*" she exploded, and took off running toward the barn.

Mitch, the youngest of Andi's three older brothers, turned around as she passed him and yelled sharply. "Andi!"

Andi ignored him and kept running. She had to get away from all those watching eyes.

Stumbling into Taffy's stall, she wrapped her arms tightly around her horse's neck and sobbed. Taffy stood still, appearing to somehow understand her mistress's distress. Andi stroked the palomino's neck, sniffed back tears, and hugged her again.

"Andi . . . ?" It was Mitch's voice.

"Go away." She quickly rubbed her face against her shirt.

Mitch leaned over the half door of Taffy's stall and shoved his hat back. "Those were mighty strong words I heard from you a minute ago."

Andi shrugged. Tears threatened to spill over once more. Of course she didn't hate Chad. He was her brother. Why did she always say things she didn't mean?

She shoved herself away from Taffy and reached past Mitch for her horse's bridle. With a mighty yank, she pulled it from a nearby hook and began to put it on her horse. Her fingers shook with anger and humiliation. "He shamed me, Mitch. He shamed me in front of the entire ranch."

"Can you blame him?" came the quiet reply. "You should have seen his face when he saw you near that stallion. He was scared."

Andi glanced up from adjusting Taffy's bridle. "Yeah. Scared I'd ruin his precious horse by giving it a lousy lump of sugar."

"That's not true, and you know it," Mitch replied with a hint of anger. Then he sighed. "It's time you faced the facts, sis. You came mighty close to tragedy today. You need to slow down and think things through a bit."

Andi gathered up the reins and shoved the stall door open without replying. She knew Mitch was right. It just hurt too much to admit it. She pushed past her brother and led her horse out of the barn and into the bright morning sunshine. She mounted in one smooth motion by grasping the cream-colored mane and sliding onto Taffy's bare back.

Once she left the yard, she urged Taffy into a full, breakneck gallop. The wind tore against her face and ripped apart her carelessly braided hair, sending it streaming out behind her like the dark mane of the stallion she had so recently left.

If only Justin were here! Andi wailed silently. *He wouldn't let Chad yell at me. He'd fix everything. He always knows what to say. And he's so good at explaining things to Mother.* She cringed as she imagined her mother's likely reaction to her latest bit of foolishness.

Blinking back tears, Andi turned Taffy toward their favorite spot— a small, clear, bubbling creek up in the east pasture—and slowed her to a gentle lope. Nobody went there this time of year. It would be the perfect place to sit and think—and to stay out of trouble.

Chapter Three

LATE FOR SUPPER

A gentle nudge and the smell of sweet grass roused Andi from sleep. She opened her eyes and gazed up at Taffy. Her companion and friend towered over her like a golden giant. Andi yawned and stretched, surrounded by the grass and wildflowers of her own special thinking place. Nearby, the creek bubbled noisily.

Carelessly brushing a dark strand of hair from her face, with a sigh of contentment she clasped her hands behind her head and stared up into a sapphire-blue sky. She felt so much better whenever she came here. The sky always looked bluer up here in her meadow, and the grass greener. Even the snow-capped Sierras seemed closer.

With another deep sigh, Andi rolled over onto her stomach and propped her chin in her hands. She watched Taffy dip her nose delicately into the creek and drink slowly. The mare lifted her head and turned toward her young mistress. Clear, sparkling drops fell from her nose.

"I think I'll join you," Andi said. She rolled up her sleeves, cupped her hands, and took a long, cool drink from the stream. Beneath the surface of the water, a silver shape darted past. "Look at that fish, Taffy!" She pointed excitedly. "Wish I'd brought my pole. I could have a string of trout in no time. Wouldn't they taste good for lunch?"

Taffy nickered her response and nudged Andi, as if reminding her mistress why she was here. Andi stood up and threw her arms around her horse. "You're right. I can't fish today. I've got too much work to do." Her stomach tightened at the memory. "You're my best friend, girl," she said fiercely, burying her head in the sweet smell of Taffy's mane. "You're the only one who understands. Justin used to, but he's never around."

Andi released her hold on Taffy and threw herself down next to the creek. Picking up a rock, she tossed it carelessly into the water. "Oh, Taffy! I don't want to make everybody mad at me—it just happens." She picked up another rock and gave it a toss, enjoying the plunk it made as it hit the water. "It's no fun being the youngest. Everyone's always telling me what to do."

Five rocks later she was still trying to put the awful morning out of her mind. It was no use. She knew she couldn't stay here much longer. She had to go back, finish the stalls, and try to apologize to Chad again. *Maybe he's cooled off some by now*, she thought with little hope.

"Come on, Taffy. Let's go home." Andi pulled herself up from her favorite spot next to the creek. Her stomach gave a sudden rumble. *I wonder what's for lunch*, she mused. She mounted her horse and turned west toward home.

The brightness of the California sun struck Andi full in the face. She pulled back on the reins, puzzled. "Whoa, Taffy." She shaded her eyes and frowned. "The sun can't be going down already. It should be right overhead."

A sudden gust of cool air blew across Andi's face. She shivered. The sun *was* going down, and fast. "Oh, no!" she groaned, realizing she had slept away most of the day. There would be no chance to finish the stalls before supper. In fact, if she didn't hurry, she would be late for the evening meal.

Trouble, trouble, and more trouble, Andi moaned softly. Being on time for meals was one of her mother's strictest rules. Andi had missed the midday meal. She did not want to go without supper.

A rising tide of panic welled up inside her as she noted the sun's position once more. It would take at least half an hour of serious riding to reach the house. "C'mon, Taffy," she yelled, digging her heels into her mare's side. "Let's get going!"

Taffy galloped obediently into the setting sun for a few minutes. It wasn't long, however, before the mare slowed to a lope, then to a trot.

"What's the matter?" she asked, patting Taffy's neck. One look at her mare's heaving sides gave Andi the obvious answer. Of course. Taffy must have grazed all day while Andi slept. She knew it was unwise—even dangerous—to push her horse after such a meal. "I'm sorry, Taffy," she apologized. "Go as slow as you like." With a sinking heart, she knew she was going to be late for supper. *Very* late.

It was nearly fully dark when Andi pulled Taffy to a stop in front of the barn. Jumping down, she grabbed her horse's reins and led her hastily into the darkened building. Her conscience stabbed her like a knife as she passed the dirty stalls—one by one—on her way to Taffy's stall. She picked up a brush and was about to give Taffy her rub down, when a voice startled her.

"I'll do that for you, *señorita*."

"Diego! You scared me to death!"

"I'm sorry." The ranch hand chuckled and raised a lantern, illuminating his dark, grinning face. "You're very late. You have a lot of explaining to do up at the big house." He held out his hand for the brush.

Andi dropped the brush into Diego's hand. "I know. On top of everything else, Luisa will probably yell at me in Spanish."

Diego's smile widened. "No doubt, *señorita*. My Luisa can think of many things to say when she is upset—things you probably do not wish to hear."

Andi shrugged in resignation. "Listen, I've gotta run." She nodded toward Taffy. "You'll make sure she gets a good rubdown, won't you?"

"*Sí. Claro*—of course."

Andi waved her thanks and raced from the barn. She dashed around the house to the kitchen entrance and threw open the door. Breathless, she took two steps inside and was immediately greeted by the delicious aroma of roast beef and freshly baked bread. It made her mouth water.

"*Señorita Andrea!*" A small, round-faced, Mexican woman turned from her place by the huge cast-iron stove and regarded Andi with a look of disapproval. She shook her head and tossed a gray-streaked black braid behind her shoulder. "*Tu mamá está muy preocupada . . .*" She began to rattle off in Spanish so fast that Andi could hardly keep up with her, even though she spoke the language fluently. "Your mama is very worried about you," Luisa repeated when Andi made no reply. She placed her hands on her hips. "Where have you been?"

Andi opened her mouth to explain, but Luisa waved her into silence. "She held supper for you, but you didn't come home. Señor Chad came in awfully upset about you this afternoon. And another thing—"

Andi grimaced and headed for the sink, trying hard to ignore Luisa's scolding. Hearing her mother had held supper sent a message of hope to her gnawing stomach. If she hurried, she might make most of the meal. She gave two quick jerks to the kitchen pump and thrust her hands under the water. A few seconds later she was drying them off on a nearby towel.

Luisa's dark eyes widened. She threw up her hands in dismay. "*¡Ay, no, señorita!*" she admonished her in rapid Spanish. "That's not good enough for tonight. You get cleaned up and change your clothes before you—"

Andi cut her off with a wave of her hand. She tossed the towel onto the counter and headed for the dining room. "I'll miss what's left of supper if I do that," she replied hastily in the housekeeper's native language. "And I'm starved."

"*Señorita!* Wait!" Luisa cried out in vain. "There's company . . ." Her voice trailed off weakly as the girl disappeared.

Andi burst through the door and into the dining room at a dead run. She blurted out her apologies before looking around. "I heard you held supper for me, Mother. I'm sorry I'm late. I lost track of the time." She caught sight of her oldest brother and stopped short. "Justin! When did you get back?" With a delighted grin, she rushed over and threw her arms around his neck. "I'm so glad you're home! I've got *so* much to tell you. You won't believe what happened today. Do you know what Chad said to me?"

"Andrea." Andi spun around at the sound of her mother's quiet voice. Her smile faded when she saw a stranger sitting between Chad and Mitch. In her hurry to greet Justin, she hadn't noticed the dinner guest.

The stranger was a distinguished-looking man, with brown eyes and neatly combed silver hair. His clothes and manner shouted the words *important visitor* as clearly as if he were holding up a sign. For the first time, Andi looked closely at the rest of her family. Her mother and sister were dressed in their Sunday best. Her brothers wore suits. Her heart sank to her toes.

"Hello there." The stranger's voice broke the awkward silence. His eyes twinkled merrily at her.

Andi's face grew hot. She backed away from Justin and glanced down at herself in horror. Her overalls were grass-stained and streaked with dried mud. Her shirt hung out, wrinkled and dirty, and the sleeves were rolled up past her elbows. Her hair, which had started the day as two neatly combed braids, now hung in long, wild tangles. Small pieces of grass and flower petals speckled the dark, wavy mass, bearing silent evidence of an afternoon spent in the meadow.

Justin recovered first. He stood up, put a gentle arm around Andi's shoulder, and gave her an affectionate hug. "Jim, I would like you to meet my youngest sister, Andrea." He turned to Andi. "Honey, this is Senator James Farley—visiting from Washington. He's out west for a few weeks, making a tour of the state he's supposed to be representing." He grinned.

"I'm delighted to make your acquaintance, Miss Carter." The senator stood and gave Andi a polite nod.

"Pleased to meet you," Andi whispered quickly, not pleased at all. She made the tiniest fraction of a curtsy, which wasn't easy to do while wearing overalls. *A senator from the nation's capital,* she thought in horror. *Oh, what must he be thinking?*

Senator Farley smiled kindly and sat down. He indicated the empty seat next to Melinda. "Please join us, Miss Carter. I would certainly enjoy hearing how you spent your afternoon."

Andi turned to her mother in dismay.

"You should first make yourself presentable, don't you think?" Elizabeth offered with a slight smile.

"Yes, Mother," Andi quickly agreed. She gathered what was left of her shattered dignity and turned to Senator Farley. "If you'll excuse me please?"

The senator nodded, and Andi hurried from the room. Once out of sight, she paused briefly to hear her mother's apology and the senator's deep chuckle. "Please don't apologize, Mrs. Carter." He laughed again. "It brightened my day."

Andi waited to hear no more. She raced through the foyer and took the stairs two at a time. She slammed the door to her room and collapsed onto her bed in misery. *I'm never going back down there. Never!* She rolled over and stared at the ceiling. Her empty stomach rumbled a protest to her declaration.

The knock on her door a few minutes later startled Andi, who as yet had done nothing to make herself presentable. She sprang up, stripped off her overalls, and slipped a petticoat over her head. As she reached for a suitable dress, a second knock—more insistent this time—sounded. The door opened.

"Andrea?" Her mother walked in and closed the door behind her.

Andi sat down on her bed and let the dress fall from her hand. "Oh, Mother! How could Justin do this to me? He didn't tell us he was coming home today. And he brought a *senator*. How could he?"

Elizabeth joined her daughter on the bed. "Justin sent a telegram. It arrived just before noon. I looked for you in the barn, so I could share the good news, but you weren't there. Nobody knew where you were. I was getting worried."

That struck Andi to the heart. "I'm sorry. It's been a terrible day."

"So I've heard. Chad told me about it this afternoon. I'm shocked. But running off instead of finishing your chores didn't solve a thing, did it?"

Andi frowned. "It made me feel better."

"You're not supposed to feel better. You're supposed to learn from it, be thankful Chad loves you enough to watch out for you, and do your chores without getting into trouble."

Andi shook her head. "But he was so angry with me. I didn't know what to say. He threatened to *spank* me!" She scowled at the memory.

"I know all about it," Elizabeth reminded her daughter.

Andi hung her head. "I'm sorry, Mother. I can't do anything right these days."

Her mother was forced to agree. "It certainly appears that way." She turned her head slowly, taking in her daughter's room.

Andi followed her mother's gaze and bit her lip. Her room was exactly as she had left it—the bed unmade, yesterday's school clothes hanging carelessly over a chair, and her nightgown lying in a heap on the floor. Books and papers lay atop her chest of drawers, which stood open. A dusty saddle blanket, discarded in a corner, completed the unappealing scene.

"I hardly know what to do with you, Andrea," her mother continued. "Forgetting your chores is one thing, but disregarding Chad's instructions about the stallion is inexcusable. He's only trying to protect you."

Andi clenched her fists. "He doesn't have to be so bossy about it."

Her mother shook her head and gave Andi a firm look. "You are in the wrong on all accounts, and I want to see some improvement. *Quickly.* Do you understand?"

Andi nodded and looked at the floor.

"All right, then. Finish dressing and come down to supper." She sighed. "You can straighten your room later."

Andi's head snapped up. "I can't go down. Not with the senator there. He was laughing at me—thinking I was nothing but a dirty, silly tomboy."

Andi's mother rose from the bed. "If you don't want people thinking you're a tomboy, don't come to the table looking like one." She made her way to the door. "I expect you to be ready to eat in five minutes."

"I'm not hungry," Andi muttered.

"All right. You needn't eat. But you *will* join the rest of the family."

"Mother! Please!"

Elizabeth turned to regard her daughter one last time. "As soon as you've made yourself presentable in a manner which honors our guest, you will come downstairs and join us for supper." The look on her mother's face kept Andi from interrupting. "In this family, no one is allowed to be a coward because of a little embarrassment." She opened the door and turned for a final word. "Don't disappoint me in this, Andrea."

The door closed.

Andi was left with no choice but to do as her mother asked.

Chapter Four

EAVESDROPPER

A ndi closed her bedroom door, leaned against it, and slid weakly
to the floor. She pulled her knees up under her ruffled, laven-
der, silk dress and let out a deep sigh. "I'm glad *that's* over," she muttered. At least her stomach was full. It was the only good thing she
could say about the meal she had just left.

Even now she knew her family was enjoying dessert and coffee
with their interesting and important guest. Senator Farley had
wanted Andi to stay, but she had asked to be excused as soon as it
was polite to do so. Not another minute would she sit in embarrassed silence, with the senator grinning at her whenever he caught
her gaze. Not even the promise of apple pie could keep her at the
table when at any moment the subject of her "interesting afternoon" might be brought up.

Although Andi cared little for long, boring discussions about poli-
tics, she knew that the activities of President Hayes and the state of
the nation were safe mealtime subjects. She wasn't expected to say
anything—and she hadn't. When the talk turned to the latest Washington fashions, and Melinda peppered the senator with questions
about what the young ladies were wearing, Andi had listened and
acted like the well-mannered girl her mother expected her to be.
However, when the conversation moved around to the ranch and
Justin asked Chad about his new stallion, Andi knew it was time to
make a hasty retreat.

She spent the remainder of the evening in her room, out of sight of Senator Farley and his laughing eyes. With any luck, she could avoid him tomorrow by eating an early breakfast. She wouldn't have to sit near him in church. After that, maybe he'd be gone.

"But it means Justin will go back to Sacramento, too," she said mournfully. She didn't want that to happen—at least not until she had talked with him. If she waited long enough, Justin would come up to say good night. Whenever he was home, he made a point of spending time with his youngest sister. She had come to expect it. Tonight, she looked forward to telling her brother all about her miserable day. He would listen to her, sympathize with her, and give her the same advice her mother had given her. Somehow, it always sounded better coming from Justin.

The sound of the grandfather clock downstairs striking the hour caused Andi to look up from the book she was reading. She glanced at her own small clock. It read eleven o'clock. "What's keeping Justin?" she wondered aloud, slipping from her bed.

Andi cracked open the bedroom door and listened for the sounds of conversation coming from below. She wasn't the least bit tired, having slept away the afternoon. She crept to the top of the stairs to hear what was so terribly important that her brother couldn't pull himself away for a few minutes to say good night.

"We've got to think of something, and soon." As usual, Chad wasn't bothering to keep his voice down.

"Chad." Her mother spoke. "Your voice, please."

Chad's next words froze Andi to the banister.

"Something's got to be done with Andi, Justin," he insisted. "I've got enough on my mind this time of year without having to check up on her. I'm either redoing her chores or pulling her out of trouble most days." There was a slight pause, and Chad plowed on. "Remember what happened last week, Mitch? Sid McCoy dragged her home after he nearly ran her over with a group of geldings he was bringing in. The horses scattered, and it cost him and his men half a day's work to round them up again. I got an earful from Sid about it. When my foreman starts grumbling, I've got to listen."

Justin sighed. "It can't be as bad as you're making it out, Chad. You're always extra irritated this time of year. Give it some time."

"No. The stallion was the last straw. She could have been killed."

"It was pretty scary," Mitch admitted. "I aged ten years watching Chad creep up on her. I don't want to have to watch something like that again."

"Mother?" Justin ventured.

Andi heard her mother sigh. "I'd be grateful for some suggestions. She usually listens to you. I don't know what's come over her lately. She doesn't stop to think about the consequences—just plunges head-on into things."

"I'll talk to her," Justin replied. "But it sounds exactly like Chad at that age." He chuckled. "I remember Father getting after him all the time."

"That's not funny," Chad said. "And it's going to take more than talking. I think we should send her for a visit to Aunt Rebecca."

Andi tightened her grip on the railing until her knuckles turned white. How could Chad suggest such a thing?

"Don't be ridiculous." Justin sounded irritated. "That is definitely not an option, Mother."

"I know. Chad's just upset."

"Maybe I am," Chad replied. "But I don't think it would hurt if Andi stayed in San Francisco for a couple of months. Rebecca lives in that enormous house all alone, except for half-a-dozen servants. She's written countless times, inviting the girls for a visit. There's plenty to do and see there. If I'm not mistaken, there's a girls' school right across the street. Andi could finish up the spring term and be kept out of trouble."

"I'd be glad to go with her," Melinda offered. "I haven't been to the city in ages."

Andi blinked back tears of fury and helplessness at this suggestion. They were planning her entire future without even asking her!

"I don't think it's a good idea," Justin persisted, clearly unhappy. "There must be another solution."

"Sure there is," Chad burst out angrily. "You can take her back to Sacramento with you for a few weeks and see for yourself how much trouble she's become."

"We're getting nowhere," her mother's voice broke in. "I suggest we—"

"Eavesdroppers sometimes hear things they shouldn't." A soft voice from behind made Andi spin around in guilt and surprise. Senator Farley stood above her, gazing thoughtfully over the banister into the foyer below. She knew he couldn't see into the large sitting room, but the voices coming from it were crystal clear.

"I—I—" Andi choked on her words. A United States senator had caught her in the disgraceful act of eavesdropping on her family. She half expected the man to call out over the railing and reveal her presence or reprimand her himself.

The senator did neither. Instead, he stood quietly and regarded her with a look of sympathy. "Believe me, Miss Carter," he offered kindly, "everything will look better in the morning."

Andi could think of nothing to say. Her tongue felt glued to the roof of her mouth. Tossing all courtesy aside, she jumped up and fled to her room, shutting the door behind her. She threw herself onto her bed and dissolved into inconsolable tears.

When the tears no longer came, Andi wiped her eyes and sat up. She plucked at her coverlet, thinking hard. It was obvious she was a lot of trouble to everyone on the ranch. Until tonight, she hadn't realized just how *much* trouble.

Remembering her family's conversation, and the words *Aunt Rebecca* and *girls' school*, plunged her into gut-wrenching fear. "No one's sending me off to some girls' school," Andi decided. She clenched her fists and brought them down against the bed. "And I'll die if I'm cooped up in the city with Aunt Rebecca. How can Chad even consider it?" She shook her head sadly. "He must still be awfully sore about that stallion."

The thought of being sent to San Francisco brought fresh tears trickling down Andi's cheeks. She loved the ranch as much as anyone in her family. Nothing could take the place of feeling the sun and wind on her face or smelling the freshly cut hay. The friendly sounds of the cowboys working with the cattle or the plaintive cry of a lost calf were the sounds of home to her. She turned cold inside at the thought of staying with her spinster aunt for more than a few days. One visit to San Francisco had been enough to convince her she hated it—all those tall buildings stacked next to each other, closing her in so she could scarcely breathe. *No,* she determined fiercely, *not if I can help it.*

Ⓒ

A few hours before dawn, Andi saddled Taffy, tied up her bedroll, and slipped some supplies into her saddlebags. No one was up—not even the hired hands. The ranch lay in the quiet tranquility that comes just before a new day. Only the occasional rustling of the treetops broke the stillness. Andi glanced one more time at her home. Then she turned and led her horse silently out of the yard, through the gate, and onto the road that led southwest toward town.

She adjusted her wide-brimmed, black felt hat and pulled it securely over her forehead. It felt awkward and uncomfortable with her hair stuffed tightly inside, but she had no choice. She knew a strong young boy had a much better chance of finding and keeping a job than a girl. Boots, overalls, and a warm jacket completed the illusion.

Andi sighed. Maybe someday she could return home—when

everybody had forgotten about sending her to Aunt Rebecca. Perhaps in a couple of weeks her family would miss her and forget about the trouble she'd been. She could start over. But for now? Well, she couldn't get into trouble if she wasn't around. Chad couldn't boss her and tell her what to do all the time. She would be free.

She mounted the palomino and took a firm grip on the reins. "Come on, Taffy. Let's get out of here."

She didn't look back.

Ⓒ

The two travelers had no trouble seeing their way through the mild spring night. The full moon bathed the road in silver light. Andi was familiar enough with this particular stretch of road to know there were no surprises awaiting her. She traveled it several times a week to school. It was a pleasant road, bordered on both sides by acres and acres of young orchards. Only a few short weeks ago the trees were bursting with blossoms. Now all that remained was a carpet of pink and white. The discarded petals glistened in the moonlight like a layer of freshly fallen snow.

The road to town was a long one. Nearly an hour passed before Andi could make out the shadows of the outlying buildings that marked the edge of Fresno. She grew alert when she entered the town. It wouldn't do to be caught—especially by the sheriff. He would drag her home in disgrace, and she'd never hear the end of it. Being caught by one of his deputies would be just as bad, so she kept a sharp lookout for any movement in the streets.

She soon discovered she had worried for nothing. The town slumbered in the quiet hours before dawn. The saloons were closed, and the shopkeepers wouldn't open at all on Sunday morning. If the sheriff and his deputies were making their rounds, they were making them someplace else. Andi heard and saw nothing.

Once through town, she turned south and gave Taffy her head. Numerous little towns dotted this part of the valley. Any one of them might hold an opportunity to make some money and find a place to stay. Unfortunately, she had never been south of Fresno before. She had no idea how far the next town actually was.

Fresno was a fair number of miles to the north when night began to give way to a pale, cloudless dawn. Andi yawned and tried to stretch. She pulled her feet from the stirrups and brought one leg up around the pommel of her saddle—anything to stay awake and get comfortable. She was tired, and the steady clop-clop of Taffy's hooves added to her drowsiness.

How far is it to the next town? she wondered. She didn't favor being seen by the stagecoach driver, who was bound to be along a few hours after the sun rose. Although it was doubtful he'd recognize her, he'd surely remember a golden palomino and a boy, if questioned by the sheriff later on.

Busy with her thoughts and half-asleep, Andi didn't notice her horse's sudden alertness. The sound of a voice caught her by surprise and brought her back to reality.

"Whoa, Taffy," she commanded softly, pulling back on the reins. She sat up and put her feet back in the stirrups. "Who's there?"

"Howdy." An invisible voice hailed her in a friendly way.

"Who's there?" Andi asked again. The moon had set, and she strained to see through the dim light of the approaching dawn. A stab of uncertainty struck her.

The owner of the voice came into sight. He was a man of medium height and build, leading a sorry-looking horse, which appeared to be lame.

"Howdy, young fella. I sure am glad to see you!" The man grinned and shoved his hat back, allowing Andi a better look at him. Friendly blue eyes in a clean-shaven face stared up at her. "This has got to be the longest night of my life."

"Howdy." Andi returned the stranger's greeting cautiously, lowering her voice to sound like a boy.

The man moved a few steps closer. "Where're you headed?"

Andi tightened the reins and backed Taffy up. She could feel her heart pounding against her chest.

"Wait, boy!" The man held up both hands in innocence. "Don't run off. I'm really stuck. My horse found a hole and went lame on me. I've been walking for hours. How far is it to the next town, do you know?"

Andi began to relax at the man's open, easygoing manner. Her heart stopped racing and she breathed easier. "It's a couple hours' riding time to Fresno, but a lot longer if you're walking. You're better off finding a place to rest alongside the road. The stage should be by in an hour or two. The driver might pick you up."

The man shook his head. "I dunno. I'd much rather get me another horse." He grew quiet.

Andi watched the stranger's gaze sweep over her horse and tack. Taffy was a fine horse—one of her family's best. Andi shifted uncomfortably in her saddle and gripped the reins with a shaky hand.

The man reached out and patted Taffy on the chest. He gave a low whistle. "Where did you get this horse, boy? Sure is a beauty."

"She's mine." Andi urged Taffy back a few more steps. The mare whinnied nervously, no doubt sensing Andi's uneasiness.

The stranger laughed and backed off. "I can see that." He folded his arms across his chest and grinned up at Andi. "You wanna sell me the horse? I'll even throw this old nag in for free." He waved toward the lame animal.

"No."

"Aw, come on, kid. I'm sure you didn't pay for her. That's a rich man's horse and tack." He came closer, and his voice dropped to a whisper. "Why else would a boy your size be riding around in the middle of the night? Did you steal the horse from your boss?" He winked. "You sure picked a fine animal. I'll give you fifty dollars—no questions asked. That's a lot of money for a boy."

Andi stared at the man, speechless. When she found her voice, it shook with alarm. "What do you mean?" She jerked Taffy around. It was long past time to get away from this drifter. "I'm not selling you my horse." She leaned forward and prepared to gallop away.

The man reached out with amazing speed and grabbed the reins. Taffy reared up in fear, but the man yanked her down. He curled his fist tightly around the bridle and looked up into Andi's terrified face. He was no longer smiling. "Get off the horse, boy. I ain't telling you twice."

Cold fear stabbed Andi like a knife. Her heart beat furiously. Not even her morning encounter with Chad's stallion had scared her as much as this stranger did.

In the space of a few frightened seconds, she came to understand her brother's point of view regarding so many things that to her own mind had seemed mean and bossy. Her mother was right. Chad was only trying to protect her from dangerous situations—like the stallion—and from dangerous people—like this one. *I'm going home,* she decided in a heartbeat.

The terror she felt at the possibility of having Taffy stolen from her propelled her into action. She yanked violently on the reins and dug her heels into Taffy's flank. "Let go of my horse!"

The mare leaped forward, but the stranger held firmly to the bridle. With his free hand, he reached out and wrenched Andi roughly from the saddle. He hurled her into the rocks and brush that lined the side of the road. She landed with a crash and lay still.

Chapter Five

NEW FRIENDS

Andi woke with a groan and tried to sit up. She felt her head explode into a thousand pinpricks. A pair of gentle but firm hands prevented her from rising, and a voice spoke in soothing tones.

"*Acuéstate, chiquita.*" The Spanish words sounded strange, yet familiar, and Andi lay down in obedience to the command. Her head immediately felt better. "*Mucho mejor,*" came a satisfied whisper.

Slowly, Andi opened her eyes, being careful not to move. Gazing down at her was the friendly, open face of a Mexican woman. Her dark eyes showed her relief at finding Andi awake.

"*Buenos días.*" The woman smiled broadly.

"*Buenos días, señora,*" Andi replied cautiously. "*¿Dónde estoy?*"

Astonishment filled the woman's face. "You speak Spanish."

"*Sí,*" came Andi's distracted reply. "Please," she repeated. "Where am I?"

"You are with the Garduño family. I am Nila. It has been many hours since my husband found you on the road. You were unconscious. He brought you here, to our camp. I cleaned and bandaged a deep cut on your head. What happened?"

Andi frowned and tried to piece together the past few hours. "I'm not exactly sure. I remember riding my horse, but not much else." She looked around anxiously. "Did you bring my horse here, too?"

"No. I'm sorry. We found only you—no horse."

"Oh, no," Andi whispered. Guilt washed over her. If Taffy was lost or stolen because of her foolish running off, she would never forgive herself. "I—I don't remember anything else."

"Not to worry, little one. It is likely everything will return in a day or two." Nila patted her gently on the arm. "If you tell us your name, we can return you to your family. They must be worried about you."

"It's Andrea."

"Andrea? That's all? Just Andrea?"

"Please, *señora*, I don't want you to return me to my family. Not yet. Not until I find my horse."

"But your *mamá*, your *papá!*"

"No. Thank you, *señora,* for what you've done already. If you'll take me back to the place you found me, I can start searching for Taffy. Please."

"But, child, you have nothing! No horse, no money, no decent clothes!" She waved a scoffing hand toward the overalls hanging over the back of the wagon. "Those are the clothes of a boy, not of a young lady."

"I know," Andi agreed. "I thought it would be safer to travel as a boy."

The woman chuckled and shook her head. "Not many would mistake you for a boy, no matter what you're wearing." She reached out and grasped a handful of Andi's tangled mass of dark waves. "Even if you were to cut your hair, it would not help, for you do not speak or act like a boy. Your speech is gracious and educated—like one would expect from a young lady of good family."

Andi stared at the woman in dismay.

"*Está bien, chiquita.* It's all right," Nila assured her. "You may stay here for the present, at least until you are fully recovered. It is unthinkable that we would allow you to wander off with no protection."

She gave Nila a grateful smile. "*Gracias.*"

"I will tell the others you have finally awakened. Would you like to meet my family? The children are very curious."

Andi nodded and closed her eyes, suddenly exhausted.

Nila sighed. "I think perhaps my family will meet you later. You must rest first and recover." She laid a cool, gentle hand against Andi's forehead and smiled. "Do not worry, little one. The Garduño family will care for you and see you safely returned to your family. That is a promise."

The sounds of laughter and play awakened Andi. She opened her eyes and found herself in the back of a small wagon, sprawled out on a bed of mounded quilts and blankets. She looked up at a grove of cottonwood trees waving slowly in the afternoon breeze, their new leaves bursting green against the sky. In the distance she could hear friendly chatter and the occasional braying of a donkey. They were pleasant sounds. Andi propped herself up on one elbow and looked over the side.

She saw a camp. Whether it was permanent or temporary, she couldn't tell. There was a fire being tended by the Mexican woman, Nila, who was frying tortillas with a deft hand. It made Andi's mouth water to look at the food, and her stomach growled.

"*Buenas tardes,*" a strange voice uttered.

Andi whirled around. A young girl not much older than herself was staring at her. "*Buenas tardes,*" Andi replied. "Who are you?"

"I'm Rosa," the girl answered with a smile. "And you're Andrea."

"That's right."

"How do you feel?"

"Much better. My head hurts only a little." She grinned suddenly. "What is he doing with that burro?" She pointed to a small gray donkey and a boy struggling with it.

"My brother is trying to hold him still long enough to get on," Rosa replied. "Joselito dreams of becoming *un gran vaquero*—a grand cowboy—someday." She giggled. "He uses our burro to practice riding. Watch!"

Andi held her breath as the boy threw himself onto the donkey's back. The little beast looked surprised for a second before kicking up its heels. Joselito flew between the burro's ears and landed facedown in the dirt. Rosa howled with laughter.

The donkey brayed and took off running.

"He's getting away!" Andi exclaimed.

"Don't worry. He never goes far. A little corn always brings him back."

"I see you are much better, *chiquita*." Nila's voice broke into the girls' conversation. She reached out and gently drew the white cloth from around Andi's head. She examined the gash, nodded in satisfaction, and replaced the cloth. "Yes. Much better. How does your head feel this afternoon?"

"I've got a headache, but it's nothing like earlier today. Thank you again."

Nila waved the thanks away. "*De nada*," she insisted. "It's nothing." She indicated the campfire. "Are you hungry? We have some fresh tortillas and beans."

"I'm starved." Andi sat up straight. Although her head still ached from her accident, it didn't make her want to stay in bed, and she wasn't dizzy. She glanced around for her overalls, but they had mysteriously vanished. "Where are my clothes?"

Nila dismissed Andi's question with a careless wave of her hand. "Your things are not suitable for a young lady. Joselito will get much better use from them than you." She smiled and held up a worn but still colorful skirt and a plain white blouse. "You may wear these for now."

Although her overalls and shirt were much more practical, Andi could hardly insult the kind woman by saying so. Instead, she nodded politely and slipped into the strange clothes.

Nila nodded her approval and offered Andi a helping hand. "Now, come."

Andi carefully made her way over the back of the wagon and onto the ground. As her bare feet touched the warm dust, she winced. Every muscle in her body ached. She steadied herself against the wagon.

"Are you all right?" Rosa asked kindly.

"I'm fine," Andi insisted, though she felt suddenly fatigued. But she couldn't lie around in bed; she had to find Taffy!

Nila led her to the fire and helped settle her onto an old fallen log. She heaped a generous portion of beans and tortillas onto a tin plate and handed it to Andi, along with a steaming cup of coffee. Her face showed her pleasure when Andi devoured the offering.

"Now that your stomach is content," another voice began, "perhaps you would be kind enough to tell us your story—who you are and where you are from."

Andi swallowed the last of her coffee and turned to look at the owner of the voice. He was a tall, middle-aged man with a mustache, wearing the loose cotton pants and shirt typical of Mexican peasants. He had a serious, honest face, and the look of one who had seen his share of hardships. He stood before Andi, waiting patiently for her reply as he chewed on a tortilla and sipped his coffee.

"Now, José," Nila warned, rising from her seat. "I told you the child must not be pestered about such things. She is recovering from a head injury."

"I only wish to know where she lives, so we can return her to her family," the man replied pleasantly.

"But—"

José lowered his cup of coffee and spoke firmly. "Wife, I do not like mysteries." He pointed to Andi. "And this young girl has been a mystery ever since I found her. It makes me nervous. We are newly come to the United States and do not understand the customs or people. We do not know who this girl is or where she's from. Such things could be dangerous." He turned to Andi, and his voice softened. "I mean no disrespect to you, *señorita,* but I would be grateful for some answers."

"*Sí, señor,*" Andi agreed quietly. "But please don't make me tell you where I'm from. I must first find my horse—my best friend."

"I see. So, you will not tell us your name?"

"It's Andrea. I told the *señora* already."

"How did you come to be on the road last night?"

"I think someone stole my horse and knocked me down," Andi replied. "It all happened so quickly. I tried to get away, but . . ." Her voice trailed off as she briefly relived the horrible memory of losing Taffy. She looked up at José. "I must find my horse before I return home. I can't go back without her."

"You are so sure of this?"

"*Sí.* I am," she answered firmly.

José swallowed the rest of his coffee and set down his tin cup. When he spoke again, his voice was gentle but firm. "Why were you not at home where you and your horse belong?"

It was the question Andi had been dreading, and the one for which she had no good answer. "I left," she whispered, bowing her head in shame.

"You left home?" José probed patiently. "Why? Were you mistreated?"

Andi shook her head. "No." Her eyes welled up with tears when she thought about how foolish she had been. "I was angry. I didn't think about what I was doing. I just ran."

"I see," José murmured in a voice that sounded as if he understood all too well.

Andi rubbed her eyes and tried to swallow the lump forming in her throat. "And now I've lost my horse!" she wailed, unable to hold the tears back any longer.

"José!" Nila cried out, rushing to her. "See what you have done!" She pulled Andi into a tender embrace and rocked her gently.

The two Garduño children watched with wide eyes, their food untouched.

José sighed. "Look at me, child." Andi looked up and sniffed back her tears. The man smiled. "I do not mean to be harsh, but it is a dangerous thing for you—a young girl—to be wandering around in the open country, alone. You belong under the protection of your family, where you are safe." He sighed again. "You are fortunate to have fallen in with us. Tomorrow morning we will take you back to your family. They will understand. A good family always does. You will be scolded, then forgiven, and all will be as before."

"It *won't* be as before!" Andi jumped up. She winced as her head protested her sudden movement. "I *can't* go back. Not without my horse. I could never hurt my brother like that. He gave me Taffy when I was six years old. It would kill him to see what I've done. I allowed my best friend to be stolen. All because I was feeling sorry for myself." She faced José and slowly shook her head. "I won't tell you where I live. Just give me my own clothes and I'll leave."

"No, child," José said firmly. "We cannot allow you to go off on your own. I see you are a stubborn girl and this horse means much to you—too much for you to see clearly." He let out a weary breath, as if regretting what he was about to say. "If you like, you may stay with us for the time being. Perhaps we will come across your horse. After all, it has been less than a day."

"*¡Gracias, señor! ¡Gracias!* You won't be sorry. I'll work hard to pay for my food. Anything you ask. And I promise when I find my horse, I'll gallop home as fast as I can and ask to be forgiven—just like the prodigal son in the Bible, except"—Andi grinned suddenly—"I'm a *daughter*."

José nodded. "*Bueno.* Now, I think there may be a way you can help us."

"How?" Andi asked eagerly.

"You speak English, *no?*"

ANDREA CARTER AND THE LONG RIDE HOME

Andi frowned at the unexpected question. "Yes."

"*¡Qué bueno!*" José broke into a broad smile. "We are at a disadvantage here in California. Because we cannot speak the language, many *gringos* cheat us when we try to buy supplies. They pay us unfairly for our work, or sometimes not at all." His look turned serious. "Would you be willing to teach us English and speak for us to the *gringos* in exchange for food and clothing—and, of course, for our aid in the search for your horse?"

Andi nodded. "*Sí, señor. ¡Con mucho gusto!*"

Chapter Six

SECOND THOUGHTS

Andi gazed across the field of beans and groaned. It looked identical to the other fields that she and the Garduño family had worked the past week.

"I got only a few days' work fer ya, that's all," a loud, hurried voice was saying. The voice belonged to a heavyset, overalls-clad farmer. He was chewing rapidly on a generous wad of tobacco, swirling it around and around in his cheek. With a practiced aim, he spat a brown stream at José's feet. He grinned and continued.

"Most o' this field's been picked already by me an' my young'ns. I'd be finishin' up if it weren't fer this bum back o' mine and the fact that the young'ns come down with the ague. Got the chills real bad." He spat again, this time at Nila's feet. "Can't pay ya much, ya understand. The missus'll give yer woman some grub fer yer family. What'd'ya say?"

José glanced down at Andi with a questioning look. In rapid Spanish, she told him all the farmer had said. José looked out across the field, took a deep breath, and nodded. *"Bueno. ¿Adónde vamos?"*

Andi turned to the farmer. "All right. Where do we go?"

The man pulled up his work-worn overalls, adjusted his slouch hat, and shot another stream of tobacco juice at José's feet. He waved a dirt-encrusted hand toward a small stand of cottonwoods about fifty yards away. "See them trees 'cross the field?"

Andi nodded.

"That's the creek. Start there an' work yer way back t' the barn. Got some wood that needs choppin', too, and a couple stalls t' be mucked out." He grinned down at Andi and Rosa. "Can ya handle a pitchfork?"

Andi bit her lip and nodded.

"And you, boy." The farmer waved toward Joselito. "You can fill the wood box fer the missus, then get out in the fields with yer folks."

"He wants you to chop wood," Andi told the boy in Spanish. "Afterward, you can join your parents."

Joselito nodded and headed for the woodpile.

The farmer squinted into the early morning sunshine. "Gonna be a hot one t'day." He turned to the small, Mexican family. "Come see me at sundown. The missus'll get ya yer grub." He frowned. "Well, what're ya waitin' fer? Get t' work!"

This time, José needed no translation. He snatched up a couple of empty bushel baskets and headed for the field. Nila followed with a basket in each hand.

"Come with me," the farmer commanded Andi and Rosa. "I gotta hitch up the team so's yer folks kin load the baskets. I'll show ya the stalls that need muckin' out."

Andi and Rosa followed the dirty farmer into a barn that looked ready to collapse. It was musty inside and dark, except for the strips of sunlight shining through wide cracks between the weathered planks. Barely four feet above their heads, a sagging loft threatened to tumble down on them. Small pieces of last summer's hay drifted through narrow cracks and into the girls' hair.

With a grunt, the farmer handed each girl a pitchfork and set a crude, broken-down wheelbarrow in front of them. Then he left them to their task.

"¡Qué horror!" Rosa exclaimed, turning a full circle. She grasped a small crucifix hanging around her neck and began murmuring quietly to herself.

"What are you doing?" Andi asked, heading toward an empty stall. "Praying?"

"*Sí*," came the fervent reply. "I'm praying this old barn holds together. Let's finish quickly and get out of here!"

Andi smiled. "I'd much rather muck out stalls in this nice, cool barn than pick beans out in the sun." She threw a forkful of soiled hay into the wheelbarrow. "I've never worked so hard in my entire life as I have these past few days. I'll sure be glad when the bean harvest is over."

"Why? You think picking lettuce or melons or tomatoes will be easier?" Rosa asked, struggling with her pitchfork.

"You don't mean . . . ?" Andi paused at Rosa's slowly nodding head.

"If *Papá* cannot find a steady job, we'll have to follow the crops in order to earn enough to live," the girl explained matter-of-factly.

Andi leaned on the pitchfork and stared thoughtfully into the dirty stall. This was not the way she'd imagined things would turn out when she'd begged the Garduño family to allow her to stay with them. She'd been confident that she would find Taffy in a day or two and be on her way home by now. Instead, she had discovered that searching for her horse could only be done in snatches—while passing through small, valley towns on the way to another harvesting job. The rest of her days were taken up with working, English lessons with the Garduños, and resting her sore and tired body.

"You want to go home, don't you?" Rosa asked suddenly, jerking Andi from her thoughts.

Andi pitched another load of soiled hay into the wheelbarrow before tossing the pitchfork to the ground. "I sure do," she admitted slowly. She picked a few pieces of hay from the skirt and blouse that Nila had supplied. She knew the Garduño family had been kind, but these weren't *her* clothes. It didn't feel right to be wearing them. "I miss my family," she confessed.

For the first time in her life, Andi felt lonely. "I miss curling up on my sister's bed and giggling over the funny things she tells me about her gentlemen callers," she continued. "I miss being invited to sit on the bunkhouse porch and listen to the cowhands' stories of the places they've been. I . . . I miss saying good night to my mother," she finished in a rush of words. She lifted the handles of the wheelbarrow and gave it a shove. It moved awkwardly toward the barn's open doors.

"*Papá* would take you home if you asked," Rosa said, putting down her pitchfork. She brushed a wayward strand of black hair from her face and followed Andi. "He's wanted to all along."

"I know," Andi replied, dumping the heavy load just outside the door. "But I have to find my horse."

"Did you learn anything yesterday in that little town we passed through?"

"Not a thing. I asked every person I met. I described Taffy's saddle and bridle, but nobody had seen her *or* that dirty, rotten, good-for-nothing horse thief that ran off with her." She mumbled the last part in angry English, and Rosa gaped at her in surprise. "Don't worry," Andi assured her. "I'm not saying anything *really* awful. I just can't think of anything bad enough to call him in Spanish."

Rosa nodded and helped bring the wheelbarrow back into the barn for the second stall. "I could. I could teach you many bad things to call him, but"—she grinned—"I'd better not."

Andi let out a long, thoughtful breath. "You know what, Rosa? Looking for Taffy is turning out to be a harder job than I figured. That thief could be clear to Nevada by now!" She thrust the pitchfork into a pile of hay. "I wonder what Chad would say if I showed up at the ranch without Taffy," she mused quietly, forgetting Rosa for the moment. "But"—she shook her head—"I've been so bad, running off like I did. The least I can do is bring Taffy back." She gave her friend a pleading look. "Right?"

"I really think you should go home."

Andi sighed. "Maybe you're right." She smiled at Rosa. "I'll think on it."

Late that night, Andi lay curled up beside Rosa on a mound of old quilts. She was exhausted from another long, hot day in the fields, but she couldn't settle down to sleep. Her body ached. Her face burned from too much sun. She felt sticky with dried sweat. She would have given just about anything for a warm bath and a plate piled high with roast beef and potatoes and gravy. The constant fare of beans and tortillas—which she'd so hungrily devoured a week ago—was becoming tiresome. Her mouth watered at the thought of a tall glass of cold milk and one of her mother's sugar cookies.

Andi tossed and turned, her thoughts whirling and spinning inside her head like a swarm of angry bees. Go home? Sleep in her own bed instead of on this hard ground? Go fishing next Saturday instead of bending over an endless row of beans? Ride like the wind across acres and acres of—

No! Her thoughts came to a screeching halt. There was nothing to ride *on*. If she went home now, she would have to accept the fact that Taffy was beyond reach. She'd have to face her brother, and she wasn't sure she could do that. Chad was bossy—so determined, it seemed, to keep her from having a good time—but she loved him. She knew Taffy's loss would hurt him deeply. After all, Taffy had been his idea, his gift to her on her sixth birthday.

She had been astonished when Chad had ripped off her bedcovers and spirited her away to the barn that spring morning long ago. Was it another one of his mean, teasing tricks? He seldom passed up an opportunity to annoy her, and she was just as often ready to challenge him back.

Yet there'd been no teasing in his bright blue eyes when he'd carefully set Andi down beside the wobbly-legged, golden filly. He had grinned at her surprised gasp and gently whispered, "Happy birthday, little sister."

Andi had stood frozen. A horse of her very own? She couldn't breathe. She didn't even blink for fear of spoiling that magic moment.

Finally, she had reached out a hesitant finger and touched the filly's soft nose. The little one had sniffed the hand, jerked her head up, and scurried to the other side of a stately, white mare. A few seconds later, the foal had poked her head out from behind her mother and stared at Andi.

"Really, Chad? She's really, truly for me? You're not teasing?"

"You bet she's yours. I'm going to teach you how to gentle her and make her your friend. You'll have one fine filly when we're finished. I promise."

Chad had kept his promise. The countless hours he'd spent with Andi and the filly had brought the three of them together in a special bond. In Andi's eyes, Taffy belonged to Chad as much as to her. She wouldn't go home without her.

She didn't dare.

Andi lay still and gazed up into a sky awash with stars. Her decision to keep searching made her feel lonelier than ever. What was her family doing right now? Were they looking for her? What about Taffy? Where was her horse? Did the drifter still have her? Was she frightened or mistreated?

Andi sniffed back a few tears and offered up a quiet prayer for her family and her best friend. *I know I don't deserve any favors, Lord, but please help me find Taffy. Not for myself, but so I can take her home, where she'll be safe.* Then she rolled over and fell asleep as dawn began to fill the sky.

Chapter Seven

A CLUE

N *ot much of a town,* Andi decided after her first glimpse of
Livingston Flats. She stood with the Garduño family at the
edge of town and let her gaze travel the length of Main Street. A
couple dozen drab, flimsy wooden buildings with false fronts lined
the dusty street on either side. The signs for a bank, a hotel, three
saloons, and a general store caught her attention. She imagined the
rest of the buildings held similar businesses. At the very end of the
street, Andi could make out the railroad depot.

In a town this small and rundown, she thought reasonably, *Taffy
should stand out like a gold nugget in a gravel bed. Certainly, someone
will remember seeing her. All I have to do is find the right person.*

"I'm going to ask around and see if anyone's seen Taffy," Andi told
Nila.

The woman nodded. "*Está bien.* José does not need you to speak
for us now. Perhaps later." She indicated her husband, who had moved
away to join a few of his countrymen in front of a small cantina.

"May I come with you?" Rosa asked. "I'd like to help look for your
horse."

"Of course." Andi grinned and held out her hand. "It would be
nice to have a friend along."

Smiling, Rosa grasped Andi's hand, and the two girls headed down
the street.

"We'll walk through town and ask anyone who happens along,"
Andi decided, skipping across the street. She was in high spirits at the
possibility of learning something about Taffy this afternoon.

The door to the two-story hotel opened, and a smartly dressed couple stepped out. Andi greeted them with a cheerful smile. "Excuse me. Have you seen a golden palomino horse with a—"

The man pulled his companion closer to his side and brushed past Andi as if she didn't exist. The couple hurried along the boardwalk and disappeared into the bank without a backward glance.

Andi stared after the couple. "They sure weren't very friendly. I wonder why." She grabbed Rosa's arm and pointed down the street. "Let's try the general store. Lots of folks are going in and out."

Andi stood outside the entrance and talked to a dozen shoppers before she realized she wasn't getting anywhere. Most of the women wouldn't speak to her at all. Those who replied to her questions did so in short, clipped sentences before hurrying away.

"I don't understand it." Andi folded her arms across her chest. "Of all the rude, sour folks I've ever met, the people of this town take the prize."

Rosa shrugged. "Your hair is dark and you're dressed like me, so they think you're Mexican."

Andi glanced down at the skirt and blouse that Nila had given her. Her cheeks grew hot in sudden understanding. She looked up at her friend and opened her mouth. No words came out.

"*Lo siento*," Rosa murmured.

Andi shook her head firmly. "No. *I'm* the one who's sorry. Sorry some folks have to act so uppity." She squeezed Rosa's hand. "Come on. Let's not let their bad manners spoil our day."

The two girls continued down the street. They passed the newspaper office, a millinery shop, and a doctor's small office without meeting anyone. Andi was ready to give up and return to the Garduño family camp when a young cowhand rode up, dismounted, and tied his horse to the railing in front of Andi.

"Hey, mister," Andi hailed the man. "Can I ask you something?"

He looked up. "Sure, missy." He leaned against his horse in an easy manner and pushed his wide-brimmed hat away from his forehead. "Shoot."

At last! A friendly fellow! "Have you seen a golden palomino mare around these parts?"

The man lost his grin and straightened up. He frowned in thought. "I might've," he said. "Describe her."

"She's about fifteen hands high, with a white stripe on her nose and four white socks. Her mane and tail are creamy white."

The cowhand looked thoughtful. "Anything else? Saddle? Brand?"

Andi nodded and dropped to her knees. With her finger, she traced a large letter C in the dusty street. Then she drew a circle around the C. "This is our brand, the Circle C," she explained quickly, dusting her hands off and rising to her feet. "The saddle is nearly new and decorated with fancy etchings."

The man was nodding at Andi's recital. "I've seen a horse like that—just last week, in fact." He whistled appreciatively. "A right pretty little filly."

"Here? In Livingston Flats?" Andi couldn't believe her good fortune. A clue at last! "Where did you see her?"

"Well . . ." He shuffled uncomfortably and glanced behind his shoulder.

Andi followed his gaze. Across the street, a sign advertising Jake's Place hung above a larger sign that read Saloon. "Go on," she insisted.

"Why are you asking all these questions?" the man asked, turning to face her.

"My horse was stolen almost two weeks ago. I've been looking for her everywhere."

"Well, missy," he said sadly. "I don't have good news for you." He pointed to the saloon. "A fella rode into town on a palomino like you described and lost her in a card game just a few hours later." The cowhand shook his head. "I only remember the incident 'cause he practically tore the place apart when he lost all his money. The whole town couldn't help but hear the ruckus. Sheriff tossed him in jail to shut him up."

"What about my horse?" Andi persisted. She didn't want to hear about that miserable horse thief.

"I don't know the fella who won her," the man continued. "He wasn't a local. I reckon he was just passing through town. I saw him mount his own horse and lead the palomino away. Haven't seen either of them since." He paused. "Have you checked with the sheriff?"

Andi shook her head. She wasn't eager to involve a sheriff in her search. A sheriff was bound to ask questions she'd prefer not to answer.

The cowhand shrugged. "Sheriff probably couldn't help you, anyhow. The drifter who won your horse is most likely long gone." He pointed down the street. "You might try the livery stable. Jon March knows just about everything that goes on in this town. Who knows? He might've boarded your horse for the night. Perhaps he even bought her. He's quite the horse trader."

"The livery stable," Andi repeated, nodding. "Yes, I'll check there." Then she smiled at the young man. "Thank you, mister."

"My pleasure, missy." He tipped his hat to Andi, nodded at Rosa, and mounted his horse. "A word of advice. Jon March can be downright unpleasant at times. Watch yourself."

Before she could respond, the cowboy rode away.

Andi raised a hand to shade her eyes from the sun and scanned the street. "There," she exclaimed. "I see the livery stable. It's just a couple of blocks away. ¡Vámonos!—Let's go!"

The girls hurried down the boardwalk and crossed the street to a large, dilapidated building with a faded sign proclaiming March's Livery Stable & Feed. An enormous set of double doors hung open, allowing light to penetrate the dim interior.

A smaller door to the left of the stables opened, and a heavily built, scruffy-looking man emerged from the shadows. When he saw the girls, he planted his meaty fists on his hips and scowled.

"Are you Jon March?" Andi asked.

The man gave Andi a curt nod and pulled a pipe from between clenched teeth. "I ain't got no jobs for hire," he declared. "And I don't rent to your kind."

Andi frowned at the man's rudeness. "I'm not looking for a job, and I don't want to rent your horses."

"That so?" he growled, thrusting the pipe back into his mouth. He eyed the girls suspiciously. "Then what's your business?"

"I'm looking for a horse you might have boarded here a week ago. A golden palomino mare about fifteen hands high."

The man's eyes widened, and Andi paused. Then he cleared his throat and muttered, "Nope. Haven't boarded nuthin' like that. Now, get outta here."

"But I've barely described her," Andi argued, taking a determined step forward. "If you'd just let me finish, maybe you'd remember—"

The owner of the livery closed the distance between himself and Andi and pulled the pipe from his mouth. His hand shook as he jabbed the stem toward Andi. "Listen, girl, and listen good. I haven't boarded the horse you're describing. Not last week. Not any week."

"May I look inside your stable?" Andi asked.

"No!" the man snapped. "This here's private property." His eyes narrowed as he looked over the girls' shoulders. "I got a customer. Go on, now. Get off my place."

Andi didn't move. "Someone won her in a card game. She was wearing an expensive saddle and—"

The owner shoved his dirty, unkempt face into Andi's, causing her to stagger backward. He caught her and pulled her to her feet. In a low, harsh voice he growled, "I told you I don't know nuthin' about a palomino. Now, get out of here and don't come back. If I see you around my place again, I'll have the law on you. Understand?"

Andi nodded and shook herself free of the man's grip.

Mr. March grunted and brushed past the two girls. He hailed his customer with a friendly wave of his pipe. "George! Howdy! You here for a rig? Come on in the office and we'll talk."

Andi watched the two men disappear through the small door and into the shadows. Then she fixed her gaze on the large, open doors leading to the stables. "Come on, Rosa," she said, pulling on her friend's sleeve.

"What's happening?" Rosa wanted to know. "I didn't understand any of that."

Andi quickly explained as she led her friend around to the side of the livery stable. "The owner acts like he's hiding something. He wouldn't listen to me. He wouldn't let me look at his horses. He seemed jumpy and awful anxious for us to leave." She peeked around the corner and saw March and his customer leaving the office. They headed toward a nearby lean-to, where an assortment of different sized buggies waited to be rented. "Maybe he's got Taffy in the stable. I'm going to find out."

As soon as the two men were out of sight, Andi sprinted across the yard and ducked into the gaping blackness of the livery stable. She beckoned to Rosa, who crept up beside her and looked around.

"Another rickety barn," the girl murmured, shaking her head.

Andi shushed her and headed for the horses. There were a dozen stalls, most of them occupied. As soon as her eyes adjusted to the poor light, she began her search. She poked her head into each stall, talking softly to avoid startling the horses. Rosa followed close behind.

Finally, Andi reached the end of the stalls and stopped. "She's not here," she murmured. "I was so sure that man was hiding something." She leaned against the back wall and gazed down the aisle, lost in thought.

Rosa's worried voice brought Andi back. "Let's leave before he returns and finds us here."

Andi made her way toward the light, sick at heart. *Oh, Taffy! Where are you? I was so close! What do I do now?*

Not wanting to overlook any detail, however small, she crossed the open area in front of the doors and explored the other side of the livery stable. This part of the building was piled high with things needed to run the livery: hay, sacks of feed, horse tack, harnesses, spare wheels, buggy whips, tools, and saddle blankets. There were even a number of old saddlebags and canteens heaped in a corner.

Andi carefully picked through the worn and ill-kept items. She lifted aside the blankets, peeked behind a stack of empty wooden crates, and examined the sorry assortment of saddles. Then she knelt in the corner and began digging through the clutter of saddlebags and canteens.

"What are you looking for?" Rosa whispered, glancing nervously toward the open doors.

"A clue. Anything to prove Taffy was here." Andi tossed a canteen to the side and sighed in defeat. "But it looks like this is another dead end." She blinked back tears and stood up, giving the pile of goods a frustrated kick. One set of saddlebags went flying and landed beside Rosa with a thud.

Andi spared it a brief glance before turning to leave. She was so discouraged. *Where do I go from here?* She reached down to return the bags to the pile and frowned. Her heart skipped a beat. "Rosa!" she exclaimed in a low whisper, "I think I found something."

She dropped to her knees and pulled her friend down beside her. With shaking hands, she turned the saddlebags over and nearly shouted, "Look!" Carved along the edge of the flap were the letters AC. "My initials!" Andi whooped in excitement.

She tore it open and groped inside. Empty! Quickly, desperately, she grabbed the other saddlebag and lifted the flap. She reached inside. Her fingers closed around something hard and crusty—an old, dry chunk of bread. Ugh!

Another quick search brought a reward. She pulled a smooth, stiff paper from the depths of the bag and caught her breath. It was part of a photograph. Half of it had been ripped away, as if the searchers had seen it and tried to discard it.

"It's my family," Andi whispered, stuffing what remained of the photo inside the waistband of her skirt.

"Anything else?" Rosa wanted to know.

Andi opened wide the saddle bag and peered inside. She shook her head. "Wait a minute. There *is* something more." She drew out three small coins. "Thirty cents."

Rosa's eyes widened. "We're rich."

Chapter Eight

A DIME'S WORTH
OF TROUBLE

A ndi gathered up the saddlebags and stood up. "Come on, Rosa, let's get out of here."

"You're not taking those things with you, are you?"

"Why not? They're mine." Andi slung the bags over her shoulder. She took a few steps toward the exit and froze. The rough sound of boisterous laughter and men's voices filtered through the livery stable's thin walls. Andi recognized the voices at once. Jon March was returning! "Maybe you're right, Rosa," she whispered, dropping the saddlebags where she stood. Frantically, she searched the shadows for another way out of the stable. Nothing. No windows. No back door.

Rosa clutched her arm. "Let's hide!"

Andi nodded. As quietly as she could, she led Rosa through the maze of cast-off equipment, barrels of metal parts, and stacks of crates. She shuddered, imagining the livery owner's fury if he found them trespassing inside his barn.

"I'll get the horses and hitch up your rig. Won't take but a minute," Jon March shouted. He entered the stable at a brisk walk.

Andi ducked behind some hay bales, pulling Rosa beside her. She flattened herself against the prickly alfalfa and held her breath as she listened. An eternity later, she peeked around the hay and watched two large, bay horses being led outside. She let out a sigh of relief and tapped her friend on the shoulder. "Let's go," she mouthed silently in Spanish.

Without a sound, they crept from their hiding place and darted through the open doors into the sunshine. They didn't stop running until they were all the way to the general store.

"I think we got away." Andi drew in huge gulps of air. "Let's rest." She threw herself onto a crude wooden bench in front of the store and leaned her head against the large glass window, breathing deeply. "That was close."

Rosa agreed. "But your horse . . ."

"She was *here*, Rosa. That's something. I'm getting closer." She glanced toward the open doorway of the general store. "Why don't we go inside and look around? We've got thirty cents, you know."

"Should we spend so much money, *amiga?*"

Andi bit her lip. The Garduño family had very little money—certainly not enough to spend on a foolish whim. She knew she should turn the money over to José, who would use it to buy the things his family so desperately needed. *Still . . .*

"Is there anything you ever wanted to buy, if you had a few pennies of your own?"

Rosa stared at Andi. Slowly, she nodded. "*Sí.*" She reached around and pulled her long, black braid over her shoulder, twirling it around her finger in embarrassment. "I've always wanted a ribbon for my hair. A red ribbon." She sighed wistfully.

Andi pulled a dime from her skirt pocket. "We can easily buy a red ribbon with this dime and have plenty left over for a fistful of licorice besides. I'll give the other twenty cents to your father." She stood up and beckoned Rosa. "Come on."

When they entered the store, Andi nudged her friend. "It's time to practice the English I've taught you this past week." Rosa turned pale. Andi laughed and held out a spool of red satin ribbon. "You go up to the shopkeeper and say, 'I would like one yard of ribbon.' Then we'll pick out the licorice. Here. Take it."

Rosa took the spool of ribbon with a shaking hand. Andi followed her to the counter, prodding her in the back several times when the girl stalled in fear.

"You can do it," Andi whispered in her ear when they reached the counter.

The storekeeper was a round-faced man with a balding head and a handlebar mustache. Tufts of hair stuck out over his ears. He greeted Andi and Rosa with a smile. "What'll it be, girls?" he asked kindly.

Rosa swallowed nervously and set the spool of ribbon on the counter. "I like . . . *would* like . . . ." she stammered. Andi nudged her. Rosa began again. "I would like one yard rib . . . rib . . ." She turned to Andi. "*¿Cómo se dice—?*"

They were interrupted by the arrival of three fashionably dressed young ladies. A tall, pretty, brown-haired girl squeezed her way between Andi and Rosa, shoving them rudely aside. "Mr. Martin, I need these things right away," she demanded in a loud voice—a voice clearly used to being obeyed. She slid a piece of paper across the counter. "My father is expecting me home soon. Fill this order as quickly as you can." She waved a careless hand at Andi. "Get away from me. Both of you. You can wait outside until I'm finished."

Andi didn't move.

"Oh, Felicity!" A blonde girl broke in with a laugh. "They don't speak English."

Andi was so angry that for a moment she couldn't speak English or anything else. Then she snatched the ribbon from a bewildered Rosa, slammed it down on the counter, and carefully laid her dime next to it. "One yard of ribbon," she said, locking gazes with the storekeeper. "And five sticks of licorice."

Mr. Martin shook his head sadly and gave his attention to an obviously furious Felicity. "I'll prepare your order right away, Miss Felicity."

Andi watched in stunned silence as Mr. Martin bustled around the store. He wrapped the order in brown paper and tied it up with some string. "That'll be a dollar and fifteen cents."

Felicity leaned across the counter to press the coins into Mr. Martin's waiting hand. "You'd do well to be extra careful, Mr. Martin," she confided in a low voice. "They'll steal you blind when your back's turned." She gave Andi a scornful look. Then, with a flounce of her skirt, she pranced out of the store.

Andi's cheeks burned. She didn't care about Rosa's English lesson. She didn't care about the red ribbon. "I don't want this ribbon after all, mister," she decided, pushing the spool toward Mr. Martin. She had a sudden, terrible urge to chase after the girl named Felicity and slap her.

The shopkeeper nodded, as if he could read Andi's thoughts. "Miss Felicity can be . . . difficult." Quickly, he cut a length of ribbon and handed it to her. "No charge." He smiled his apology.

Andi took the ribbon with a slight nod of thanks. She gave it to Rosa and whispered, "I've had a bellyful of this town. I'm *glad* Taffy's not here any longer. Let's find your parents and leave this place."

In a town the size of Livingston Flats, it didn't take the girls long to find the Garduño family. They stood right where Andi had left them earlier in the day, near the edge of town. Nila waited quietly, watching the farm wagons and townsfolk pass by. Joselito was scratching behind the burro's ears, murmuring to the small beast as it stood harnessed to the wagon. A few yards beyond the group, José appeared in earnest conversation with a countryman.

Andi hurried over and perched herself on the side of the wagon to listen.

"Listen, *amigo*," José was saying. "My family is looking for steady work. Have you heard of anything around these parts?"

Andi wondered how many times José had asked that question this afternoon. By the look of desperation on his face, she guessed it was a lot. For their sakes, Andi hoped the Garduños could find a job. Their supplies were getting alarmingly low, and Andi knew the thirty cents she planned to give José wouldn't buy more than a few pounds of beans. Andi had an uneasy feeling that if they didn't get a job soon, she would be forced to admit defeat and go home. José certainly couldn't afford to feed an extra mouth much longer.

"Depends on how particular you are, *amigo*," the other man answered with a thoughtful frown.

"We're not particular," José assured him. He waved toward the wagon. "My family and I will do anything. Even a steady harvesting job would be welcome—one where we can stay in one place for longer than a few days."

Andi cringed at that. *Please! No beans*, she begged silently.

"Speak any English?"

"Not much," José admitted. "But there are some in my family who do." He glanced briefly at Andi.

"Well . . ." The man scratched his chin and shook his head, as if unwilling to offer more information.

"*Dígame*—tell me!" José insisted.

"There might be work out at the Lazy L Ranch."

"What kind of work?"

"Hard work," the man replied evasively.

"Could you tell me more, maybe?" José asked.

"I could, I guess, but I don't recommend it. The Lazy L is not the best place to work. *Señor* Livingston—the *patrón*—pays well, but he is a hard taskmaster and very difficult to please—especially if you're Mexican." The man's expression grew angry. "I wouldn't let my *horse* work for them, much less my family. They are cruel to their beasts."

Andi watched José digest the man's advice. He didn't seem concerned about the working conditions. The words "pays well" had made his whole face light up.

"What work, *amigo*?" José persisted.

"They are in need of a cleaning woman. The last one couldn't get along with the housekeeper. She's an old woman who's run the place for years. If you can't get along with the *Señora* Nelson, you're out."

"My wife could clean," José murmured softly.

The man continued. "They always need harvest hands. The foreman out there isn't too bad, for a *gringo*."

"*Sí*, of course." José grinned. "I must go there at once before others seek out the positions." He took a step toward his family. "Wife! We are—"

The man smiled and tugged on José's arm. "There's no rush, *amigo*. Livingston Flats is a slow-moving town. They haven't had a cleaning woman up at the house for a couple of weeks. I wouldn't let *my* wife do it."

"Perhaps your wife is not as hungry as mine."

"It may be so, *amigo*." The man laughed and gave José a friendly slap on the shoulder. "There is also a job for a girl who can speak some English. A pair of young legs to fetch and carry for the *señorita* and the housekeeper. The last girl was thrown out a week ago."

"Why?" José inquired.

"They say she was caught with one of the *señorita's* handkerchiefs. A small thing, to be sure, but the *señorita* was enraged. They say she is even harder to please than her father." He shrugged. "No one stays long on the Lazy L. You will find this out for yourself if you go there. Still, you asked me if I knew of a place that would hire you, and I have told you what I know."

José nodded. "*Gracias, amigo*. I am grateful for all you have told me. Could you give me directions to this *rancho*?"

"*Sí*."

José was in high spirits all the way back to their small camp. "We shall make such an impression on the Livingstons," he said cheerfully, "that the *patrón* cannot help but hire the Garduño family. We will work hard, mind our own business, and give him no call to find fault with us or our people." He waved toward a small, bubbling creek. "There is water. Wash yourselves. Wash your clothes. Tomorrow morning we go to the Lazy L!"

Chapter Nine

THE LAZY L RANCH

The next morning, Andi found herself standing with the Garduño family on the porch of the Lazy L, waiting for someone to answer the door. Just glancing around this fine-looking ranch—the two-story white house with freshly painted green shutters, the well-kept barns and outbuildings, the acres of irrigated pastureland—made Andi's heart squeeze with homesickness. Her determination to keep searching for Taffy was again being tested. She swallowed the lump in her throat and stared at the porch swing. *A few more days,* she thought. *I can hold out for a few more days. I'll ask the cowhands here about Taffy. Maybe they know something the livery stable owner wouldn't tell me.*

The front door opened abruptly, and Andi jumped in surprise. A tall, silver-haired woman scowled at them. She tapped her foot impatiently and spoke. "Yes? What do you want?"

Andi winced. The woman's Spanish was terrible. How would they ever understand her?

José bowed respectfully. "We are the Garduño family. I heard in town you needed a cleaning woman."

The woman gave a curt nod. "Yes. That's true." She eyed each member of the family carefully, as if her piercing gaze would uncover any dark secrets. Apparently satisfied, she nodded again. "I am Mrs. Nelson, the housekeeper." She motioned to Nila. "I am worn out trying to keep this place in order. Mr. Livingston has instructed me to find a replacement as soon as possible. I will allow you to work for a few days. Then we shall see."

Nila's face lit up. "*Gracias, señora*. You will not be disappointed."

"What about the others?" Mrs. Nelson asked.

"My son and I hope to work in the fields, *señora*," José replied. "And my . . . *daughters* . . ." He cleared his throat nervously. "Perhaps you need young servants who are light and quick on their feet to run errands for you? Both girls are used to hard work."

I am now, Andi added with a quiet sigh.

"These girls are too young," Mrs. Nelson decided with a frown.

"That may be true, *señora*, but Andrea speaks English." He prodded her forward. "You are looking for such a one, *no*? To wait on the *señorita*?"

"Is this true?" Mrs. Nelson asked in English, giving Andi a hard look.

Andi smiled and replied, "Yes, ma'am." It was such a relief to hear words that didn't sound cracked or broken.

"Humph," Mrs. Nelson snorted. "A Mexican speaking decent English—I should live to see the day." Her gaze met Andi's and held it. "You might do as a maid to Miss Livingston—in addition to other duties of course—but understand this: being a maid for the young mistress of this house is an important position. She was displeased with the last girl. Your English must be better than what she's put up with in the past. What do you have to say?"

"She won't be disappointed," Andi answered cheerfully. "I can understand anything she says."

Mrs. Nelson's gray eyes opened wide as she listened to Andi's reply. A small smile cracked her face, and her voice took on new warmth. "Very good." She turned to Nila. "I will allow you and your daughters to take the positions on a trial basis." She nodded at José. "Find Clem, the foreman. He will find you work, and he speaks Spanish."

"*¡Gracias, señora! Muchas gracias.*" José bowed.

Mrs. Nelson turned her back on José and waved Nila and the girls into the house. "Mr. Livingston is giving an important dinner party tonight, and everything must be spotless. You have arrived at the Lazy L in good time." She led her new help into the kitchen, then turned and regarded them with a critical eye. "This is a proud home, and I will have no one disgracing it. The servants who work here are quiet, submissive, and quickly obedient to Mr. Livingston, his daughter, and me. Do you understand?"

Barely, Andi confessed silently. She wished Mrs. Nelson would speak English. Nila and Rosa looked confused, but nodded at the housekeeper's words.

"Good." Mrs. Nelson brought out a tarnished silver tea service and placed it on the large worktable in the center of the kitchen. "You two"—she indicated Nila and Rosa—"get to work polishing the silver." She glanced at Andi. "You, come with me."

Andi followed the housekeeper into the dining room, where the woman waved an arm to indicate the table. "Your task, Andrea," she explained in English, "will be to set this table for the evening meal. There will be eight people in all, and it will be a formal dinner. Have you ever seen a table set formally?"

"Yes," Andi replied unhappily.

Mrs. Nelson's eyebrows shot up, and she said skeptically, "We'll see about that. The last girl didn't know the difference between a salad fork and a spoon!"

Andi made no reply.

"All right, child, let's see what you can do. Set the table immediately. When you finish, we'll see about meeting your new mistress."

"You want me to set the table for a dinner party at ten o'clock in the morning?" Andi asked, astounded.

Mrs. Nelson turned around and glared at her. "I want obedience without foolish questions."

Andi gulped back her surprise and nodded.

The housekeeper turned and left the room.

Setting the table was not her favorite task at home, so Andi had learned to do it quickly and correctly. In a short time the plates, knives, forks, spoons, glasses, and napkins were in their appropriate positions. She hurried back to the kitchen, where Nila and Rosa were busy at work, polishing the tea set.

"I like polishing the silver!" Andi exclaimed, taking a seat next to her friend. "Would you like some help?" She picked up a rag and the silver polish. "When my sister, Melinda, and I polish the silver together, we have the best time. She tells me the funniest stories about the young men who come calling." She grinned at the memory, forgetting for a moment her intention of keeping her origins a secret from the Garduños. "Once, when Jeffrey Sullivan was trying to impress her, he fell backward right into the horse trough! Wish I'd been there to see it. I would've pushed him in myself. He thinks he's so smart!"

Rosa giggled. "You would really do such a thing?"

"Oh, sure! Jeffrey needs a good dunking now and again. He's so moonstruck over Melinda, he can't see straight. My brother Mitch says cold water is just the thing to cool Jeffrey off and bring him to his senses. He told me the next time I . . ." She paused and glanced down at the rag in her hand, suddenly lost in thought. Her smile faded.

"Next time, what?" Rosa urged, clearly enjoying this amusing story of Andi's family.

"Uh . . . nothing." Andi rubbed hard on the silver.

An uncomfortable silence fell.

"You miss your family, don't you?" Nila asked gently.

Andi put down the silver sugar bowl and sighed. "Of course I do. I'd give anything to go home right now." Then she set her lips firmly. "But what I want doesn't count. I can't go home until I find my horse."

"It's only a horse."

"No. I told you how it is. I've done everything wrong. Everything! I can't face my brother without Taffy."

"Can't?" Nila asked, "or *won't*?" When Andi didn't answer, the woman continued. "Are you sure it's not your own stubborn pride that's keeping you from going home? If you think about it for one minute, *chiquita,* you'll realize your family is only interested in finding *you,* not your horse. You've been gone a long time."

Andi turned her head away, so Nila could not see the tears welling up in her eyes. She picked up the sugar bowl once more and polished furiously.

Mrs. Nelson entered the kitchen just then, preventing any further conversation. She reached out and grabbed Andi roughly by the arm. The sugar bowl clattered to the floor. "This is not your job. Go back at once and finish the table."

Andi bent down and picked up the sugar bowl. She placed it in the housekeeper's outstretched hand. "But the table is all set."

"We'll see about that," the woman snapped. She beckoned Andi to follow, and they entered the dining room. The expression on Mrs. Nelson's face turned from annoyance to joy at the sight of the perfectly set table. She clasped her hands together in surprise and favored Andi with a rare smile. "Very good, Andrea. Very good indeed. You may be a girl I can work with, after all."

"Thank you. Now, may I go back and help with the silver?"

Mrs. Nelson took a deep breath. "I'm afraid not. You must come with me. It's time to meet your new mistress."

Chapter Ten

ANDI'S NEW JOB

I told the young miss I found her a new maid," Mrs. Nelson explained, leading Andi through the Livingston house. "She wasn't pleased with the news. She has her own ideas of what a maid should be. So far, neither her father nor I have been able to find one to satisfy her."

Andi followed the housekeeper up a long flight of stairs, down a wide hallway, and into a lavish room full of ruffles and lace. She stopped and gasped in amazement. Yards and yards of satin and fine silk lay strewn across the beautiful mahogany four-poster bed, like so many discarded rags. An enormous trunk rested on its side in the middle of the room, the contents spilling onto the floor in disarray. Across the room, next to an open wardrobe, stood a mahogany bureau. Every drawer was open. Most of the clothes had been tossed onto the floor to join the rest of the confusion. A dozen or so carelessly stacked dishes rested atop the dresser, giving the room a final touch of disorder and chaos.

"I haven't time to keep her room looking nice these days," Mrs. Nelson whispered. "That will be your job."

"No wonder she can't keep a maid," Andi muttered in disgust. Her heart sank at the size of this new task.

A sudden scuffling noise caught Andi's attention.

"Whatever are you doing?" Mrs. Nelson demanded, placing her hands on her hips.

"I . . . can't . . . find it!" A high, screechy voice came from under the bed. Suddenly, amid a great deal of banging and complaining, a girl about Melinda's age rose from the floor and peered over the top of the bed. Her cheeks were flushed, and her fine, brown hair tumbled around her narrow face in wild curls. Her hazel eyes flashed with annoyance. "I've looked everywhere!" she shouted.

"That's obvious," Mrs. Nelson observed dryly. She pushed Andi forward. "I found a girl to see to your needs and keep your room straightened. Andrea, meet Miss Felicity Livingston."

For one horrible moment, Andi thought she was going to be sick. Her palms grew sweaty and she felt the blood rush to her head. She swallowed hard. "We've met."

Felicity straightened up, shook out her riding skirt, and stared at Andi. "What do you mean? Where could I have possibly met *you*?"

Andi stared stonily at the older girl. "Yesterday. At the general store."

Felicity frowned. Then her face broke into a satisfied smile. She chuckled. "Indeed, we have met," she agreed, nodding. Her eyes gleamed with interest. "For once, Agatha, you've managed to find me a housemaid I can work with. The last girl was a silly, empty-headed little thing. I couldn't get her to do anything I told her. Her only English words were *Yes, Miss* and *No, Miss.*"

Mrs. Nelson smiled tightly at Felicity's comments. "As you can see, this girl speaks English quite well."

Felicity grunted. "So she does." She picked up a dress from her bed and tossed it to Mrs. Nelson. "I want this for the dinner party tonight. Make sure each of the pleats on the underskirt is properly pressed." She waved the housekeeper away. "That will be all. I want to instruct my new maid in her duties."

"As you wish, Miss Felicity." Mrs. Nelson gathered up the yards of fabric and left the room.

Coming around the bed, Felicity approached Andi. She lifted one of Andi's thick, dark braids and gazed into her face. "I remember you. I also remember how you tried to get Mr. Martin to help you instead of standing aside politely and letting me go first, which is the proper thing to do. You are an impudent girl and need to learn your place." She smirked. "I shall be more than happy to instruct you."

Dread swept through Andi. *I bet you will,* she thought.

Felicity frowned and let Andi's braid fall back into place. "I guess you'll do. You're not as bad looking as the last girl. And at least you don't stink."

Andi felt her cheeks burn at the comment. Her hand tingled with the desire to slap the girl's haughty, sneering face, but she wisely said nothing.

Felicity laughed. "You must do everything I say and always act respectfully toward me and my family. Remember, you're in America now. If you don't like it, you can always go back to Mexico. But while you're here, *I'm* the boss." She paused, as if expecting a response. "I'm speaking to you, girl."

"Yes, Miss Felicity." Andi swallowed her disgust with difficulty and forced her tightly clamped fingers to relax.

"Good. Now, your duties." Felicity waved her arm across her room. "My bed is to be made up daily and my room cleaned. You will set out my clothes for dinner and any special event. My riding clothes, especially, must be ready whenever I want them. You will bring my breakfast up to my room at precisely nine o'clock each morning." She took a deep breath. "You won't be having any free time. I can always find something for you to do. If nothing else, you can brush my horse."

"Yes, Miss Felicity." Andi looked at the floor.

"Now, girl, the first thing—"

"My name's Andrea."

Felicity grabbed Andi by one of her braids and gave it a hard jerk, sending her to the floor with a crash. "You must never interrupt me. Is that clear? I won't stand for any of your sass."

Andi jumped up, clenched her fists, and took a step in Felicity's direction.

Felicity smiled at Andi's reaction. "So, you're one of those uppity servants, are you? You think because you speak English you're as good as Americans? You'll learn your place around here very quickly." She indicated her room. "Get to work. I want this room cleaned up, my bed made, and these awful dishes removed. Later, I will need help dressing for dinner." She paused, waiting for Andi's response. "Well?" she finally demanded.

Andi gave the girl a curt nod.

"Answer me."

"Yes, Miss Felicity," she managed.

"I'm doing you a favor by allowing you to work for me, you know. If you displease me or give me any back talk, you'll feel the sting of my riding crop—if I ever find it." Her face contorted into an impatient scowl. She resumed her search for the missing item, ignoring Andi as one might ignore a fly.

"Is this what you're looking for?" Andi asked a few minutes later. She held up a long, wicked-looking riding whip. The ends were frayed, indicating much use.

Felicity snatched the crop from Andi's hand. "Where did you find it?"

"Right here on the window sill, leaning against the curtain."

"Now I can go riding," Felicity murmured with glee, flicking her wrist. The whip whistled as it flew through the air. It connected with the bedpost with a loud crack.

Andi jumped at the noise. "You don't really hit your horse with that thing, do you?" She was appalled at the idea.

"Of course I do, you ignorant peasant. How else do you make a stubborn animal obey?" She laughed. "Right now I've an extra-willful horse on my hands. I plan on showing the beast who the real boss is." She left, slamming the door behind her.

Andi ran to the window and watched Felicity head for the large barn. The girl passed a corral where four fine-looking horses stood quietly. As soon as they saw Felicity, the horses bunched together and headed for the other side of the corral. Felicity raised her whip and brought it down across the top railing.

"You did that on purpose—just to frighten them," Andi shouted, knowing Felicity couldn't hear her.

The horses scattered in a panic, whinnying and neighing their distress. Felicity disappeared into the barn.

Andi turned away from the window and made her way to Felicity's bed. Angry and aching inside, she sat down and slowly looked around the room. The similarity between Felicity's room and her own bedroom back home hit her like a bolt of lightning. She felt not only a sharp pang of regret, but also a grim sense of justice. What she had sown in irresponsibility back home, she was now reaping in abundance.

She reached into her waistband and pulled out the torn and wrinkled photograph of her family. "I'm sorry, Mother," she whispered regretfully to the woman in the picture. "I'll never, *never* think I'm being treated unfairly again—not as long as I live. Chad was right. I've been nothing but trouble lately." She looked up at the ceiling. "I haven't obeyed *You* very well either, Lord, running away like I did. What was I *thinking*?" She stuffed the photograph back in her waistband. "I'm no better than Felicity."

Determined to make the best of a bad situation, Andi got up from the bed and began the unpleasant task of straightening Felicity's room. It wasn't easy. It took the rest of the day. While she was sweeping up the final bit of dirt, Felicity entered and began to undress. She tossed her old clothes onto the freshly made bed.

"Is my dress pressed?" she demanded.

Andi nodded. "Mrs. Nelson hung it up a few minutes ago."

Felicity threw open her wardrobe doors and examined the rich dark-green silk dinner dress. She ran her fingers along the cream-colored picot trim and nodded her approval. "First you must help me with my corset," she directed, tossing the undergarment onto the bed. "It must be laced just so."

Andi did as she was told. As she tightened Felicity's corset, she wondered for the hundredth time why anyone would want to wear something tight enough to make breathing difficult. Melinda had just recently begun wearing one, but only for special occasions. Andi intended to avoid this particular part of growing up for as long as she could.

"Now the hoops," Felicity commanded, breaking into Andi's thoughts. "And my petticoats. The train on this dress must rise in the back exactly right or it will look dreadful." Yards and yards of rich, flowing fabric settled around the girl. She attached a piece of gathered lace to her throat and shook out her full overskirt. Felicity suddenly looked years older than Melinda.

"Here." Felicity handed Andi a brush. "One hundred strokes should be good enough." She sat down and picked up a book.

Andi looked wearily at the brush in her hand and sighed. She began to brush the girl's long hair.

". . . ninety-eight . . . ninety-nine . . . one hundred," Andi finished, tossing the brush onto the vanity.

"What? Are you sure you counted correctly? I've hardly finished this chapter."

"I count very well, Miss Felicity," Andi answered, an edge in her voice. She was tired and hungry. She wondered when she could join the Garduño family for supper.

"Maybe not as well as you think. Here, take the brush and count out loud this time so I can hear you."

Andi had no choice but to begin anew. Her arm ached by the time she finished.

Felicity closed the book with a sudden bang. "My goodness! Look at the time! You're as slow as molasses, girl. My dinner guests will be arriving any moment. You'd better learn to do things more quickly. Go on, now. Leave me alone." She turned toward her vanity, her fingers flying to arrange her hair.

Andi quietly made her way past the girl. When she reached the door, she paused and looked at Felicity. "I'm sorry I don't meet with your approval," she said in her best company voice. "But you're the one who made me brush your hair twice. If you're late for your guests, it will be your fault, not mine."

Felicity's mouth dropped open. "Why you impertinent little—"

"Excuse me," Andi interrupted, giving the girl a curtsy that would have made her mother proud. "I really must be going." Before Felicity could recover from her surprise, Andi turned and made a hasty exit, shutting the door quietly behind her.

Chapter Eleven

AN UNPLEASANT EVENING

O nce out of Felicity's sight, Andi stomped down the stairs. She was boiling mad. "Patience," she warned herself. "I've got to have money to live on until I find Taffy. I've got to have a job to make some money. Things could be worse." But she didn't know how.

She was so busy trying to cool her blazing anger that she didn't notice the huge form of a man coming toward her until she ran right into him. She stumbled and fell backward.

The man caught her and balanced her against the wall. "Who are you?" he barked. "Don't you know better than to run into people? Where are your manners?"

Andi stared at the man, speechless. He was the largest person she had ever seen. He towered over her like a giant. His eyebrows formed a thick, black line across his forehead, reminding Andi of an ogre she had once read about in a fairy tale. She swallowed nervously.

"She's my new maid, Papa," Felicity offered from the top of the stairs. She glided down the staircase and came to stand next to her father.

Randle Livingston's voice and expression softened immediately at the sight of his daughter. "Well, she sure is clumsy. Let's hope she's an improvement over the last girl. Where did you find her?"

"I don't know. Agatha hired her whole family. Just some Mexican peasants."

"She doesn't look very Mexican to me," Randle observed. "I don't know any with blue eyes and freckles on their noses." He grinned suddenly and gave Andi a gentle pinch on her cheek. "Does she speak any English?"

"Why don't you ask *me*?" Andi piped up, finding her tongue at last. She rubbed her cheek and scowled at Felicity's father. They were talking about her as if she didn't even exist.

Randle regarded Andi carefully. Then he chuckled. "You have an interesting way about you—for a Mexican peasant girl. I'm sure working for Felicity will be an education." He turned to his daughter. "I hope she pleases you, sweetheart."

"She pleases me just fine, Papa." Felicity slipped her hand through her father's arm. "Now, come along. We mustn't keep our guests waiting."

"Andrea!" Mrs. Nelson's call rescued Andi from having to endure more of the conversation. She turned and headed for the kitchen. When she entered, Mrs. Nelson smiled at her. Her coldness from earlier in the day had disappeared, and she seemed ready to accept Andi as part of her capable staff. "Miss Felicity has kept you busy today, hasn't she?"

"Yes." Andi fell into a nearby chair and let out a weary breath. She glanced at Rosa, who stood at the sink washing pots and pans. Her friend looked tired, too. All in all, it had been an exhausting first day on the Lazy L. "May I go now? I'm awfully hungry."

"My goodness, no!" the housekeeper exclaimed. "I need you to help serve the table. You understand and speak English so well; you won't be an embarrassment to the Livingstons in front of their dinner guests. Quite extraordinary, your English." She favored Andi with an odd look, then went to the stove and dished some supper into a bowl. "Here. Eat this. It will revive you."

Andi accepted the bowl of food, picked up a spoon, and began to eat. The thick, hot soup was delicious, and Andi felt her spirits rise as her stomach quieted down. She studied the housekeeper while she ate. Mrs. Nelson's attitude had certainly taken a turn for the better, she decided. This morning she had seemed hard and cold; now she appeared almost friendly. She chatted freely the entire time, and Andi discovered the reason behind the woman's new attitude. Nila and Rosa had outdone themselves cleaning the house, thus lightening Mrs. Nelson's load considerably.

"And thanks to you, Andrea," she finished, "I was freed from having to tend to Miss Felicity's room and her many needs."

"How old is Felicity?" Andi asked between bites.

"*Miss* Felicity," the housekeeper reminded Andi with a frown. Then she smiled. "She turned sixteen last month. I have known her for many years. Ever since her dear mother passed away. She is high-spirited, wouldn't you agree?"

Andi shook her head. "No, I don't agree." She placed another spoonful of supper into her mouth. "She's mean and bossy and makes fun of people. Worse, she whips her horse. It's a rotten thing to do!"

Mrs. Nelson frowned. "Shame on you, child! It is not your place to criticize your betters." She wiped her hands on her apron and gave Andi her full attention. "You must learn to hold your tongue if you want to continue working here. Felicity does not tolerate disrespect from anyone—especially from a hired girl. You would do well to remember that."

Andi bowed her head. "I'm sorry. I guess I'm just tired."

"I agree." Mrs. Nelson checked Andi's bowl. "You're finished? You got enough to eat?"

"Yes, ma'am. It was very good. I feel much better."

"Thank you. I do all the cooking myself. Mr. Livingston trusts no one else in his kitchen." She smiled proudly.

"*Señora,*" Rosa's quiet voice piped up. "I am finished with the pots. What now?"

"Nothing more. You may go," Mrs. Nelson said in her fractured Spanish.

Rosa turned to Andi. "Are you coming?"

"No. I've got to serve supper to the *gringos*."

Rosa gave her a sympathetic look and then escaped out the back door.

The tinkling of a bell sounded clearly from the dining room, and Mrs. Nelson hurried toward the stove. She thrust something white toward Andi. "Quickly, Andrea! Put this apron over your clothes. You must serve the soup."

"Yes, ma'am."

"And for heaven's sake, do not say or do anything unseemly while you are serving. A servant is to be seen and not heard. Do you understand?"

"Yes, ma'am." Andi picked up the heavy tray and entered the dining room. She immediately felt disoriented. She might know how to set a formal table, but she had no idea how to serve one. At home Luisa simply put the platters of food on the table, and her family passed them around.

Afraid that at any moment she might drop the heavily laden serving tray, she crossed to the sideboard and set it down.

"Well? What are you waiting for—Christmas?" Randle Livingston's booming voice from the head of the table startled Andi into action. She began to place the steaming bowls of soup in front of the dinner guests and hoped she was doing it right. Randle sighed and smiled his apologies. "Mrs. Nelson has her hands full, training these ignorant Mexicans to do a proper job."

"Indeed!" an overly dressed, middle-aged woman wheezed scornfully. "It's so difficult to get any work out of these lazy foreigners. And they're thieves!" She raised a napkin and dabbed her lips. "Randle, didn't you dismiss your last servant for stealing?" Without waiting for a reply, she went on to slander the last maid, her family, and all Mexicans in general.

Andi listened in horror. Did the woman think she couldn't understand her? Felicity certainly knew, yet she did nothing to stop the woman's words. Never had Andi heard such shameful words about other people!

"I think this girl is doing a fine job," a voice from the other end of the table spoke up. He smiled and nodded his thanks for the soup. "*Gracias.*"

Andi looked up to see which of Mr. Livingston's guests had shown a shred of courtesy. A twinkling brown gaze met hers. Andi froze. Senator James Farley was smiling at her. Did he recognize her, or was his smile simply for a poor young Mexican girl forced to serve a table full of arrogant *gringos?*

Oh, no! Andi groaned inwardly. *He can't recognize me! Not now! I'm not ready to go home. I haven't found Taffy yet.*

The senator must have noticed her dismay, for his smile turned to a look of concern. "Are you feeling ill?" he asked in Spanish.

Andi shook her head and placed a bowl of soup in front of Felicity.

Felicity giggled at the senator's comment. "My new servant girl is such a quaint little thing, Senator. She speaks English almost as well as we do. It's so funny to hear her talk."

The senator did not appear to share Felicity's amusement. "Indeed?"

"Yes. It's quite amazing." Felicity smiled. "I believe she's been practicing. Papa says she doesn't look Mexican, so perhaps she's hoping someday to pass for one of us. Isn't that the most amusing thing you ever heard?"

"The very idea!" the middle-aged woman broke in with a gasp.

Andi watched the senator frown. Apparently he was just as disgusted with the table talk as she was.

"I'll prove it, Mrs. Thompson," Felicity said.

"I'd prefer you didn't," Senator Farley put in.

Felicity ignored the senator. "Girl, say something in English for our guests."

Andi stared at Felicity. Her thoughts spun around like a top. *Senator Farley doesn't recognize me because he doesn't expect to see me here.*

But as soon as I open my mouth he'll figure out I'm no Mexican servant girl—no matter how hard I try to act like one. Besides, I won't let Felicity treat me like a trained parrot. Quickly, she made a decision. She gave Felicity a blank look and said, *"Perdón, señorita. ¿Qué decía usted?"*

Senator Farley grinned. Felicity's face turned bright red—clearly a mixture of anger and embarrassment. Randle Livingston's face was only one shade lighter.

"Talk in English!" Felicity demanded.

Andi refused to back down. *"¿Cómo?"* She wrinkled her forehead in an expression of confusion. *"Lo siento, señorita, pero no entiendo."*

Felicity's father brought his fist down on the table with a force that rattled the dishes. "You understand very well what Miss Felicity said. And as long as you work for me, you will do what you're told, when you're told. Do I make myself clear?"

A dreadful silence fell over the room.

Andi's heart hammered against her chest. Perhaps she could stand up to Felicity, but she was no match for the furious-looking man glaring at her. She nodded her compliance.

"Good. Now bring us the rest of our meal."

Andi fled to the kitchen, her eyes burning. She slammed her fists down against the table in much the same way her employer had recently done.

Mrs. Nelson looked up in surprise. "Good gracious! Whatever is the matter?"

"I won't let Felicity treat me like that!" She went on to describe what had happened.

Mrs. Nelson groaned and wiped her hands on her apron. "Andrea, I warned you. You should have done as she asked. Instead, you embarrassed her in front of her guests." The housekeeper shook her head, clearly distressed. "Take care not to defy Miss Felicity again. The horses are not the only ones to feel the brunt of her anger."

Andi laughed at the idea. "She can't hurt me."

"You're on the Lazy L now," Mrs. Nelson said softly, dishing up platters of wonderful-smelling food. "Miss Felicity can do whatever she pleases. The last maid was a girl not much older than you. She stole a handkerchief—or so Miss Felicity says. For that, she was dismissed." Mrs. Nelson turned to Andi. Her eyes looked troubled. "She left with a stinging reminder of Miss Felicity's displeasure."

Andi considered this and quickly grew angry. "There was no call for that! Why didn't Mr. Livingston stop her?"

"It's not for you to judge your elders. I am simply warning you to be careful."

"If she comes after me with that nasty whip of hers, she'll wish she hadn't," Andi sputtered. "My brothers'll teach her some manners in a hurry and—" She broke off at the look on the housekeeper's face.

"Your *brothers*, child?" Mrs. Nelson cocked her head to one side. "I thought as much. It has not taken me long to notice that although you speak Spanish and dress like the Garduño family, you are not one of them."

"But—" Andi felt her face flame.

"You're no more Mexican than I am," Mrs. Nelson continued with a careless wave of her hand. She smiled, obviously pleased with her deduction. "Your English is flawless, unaccented. I've been watching you, ever since you set the table. You do not have the manner of a servant." She sighed. "I don't know who you are or why you are with the Mexican family. I suppose that is your own affair. But listen carefully to me. You carry yourself with the confidence and air of a fine family, and that will get you into trouble in this house. It would be better for everyone if you went back to where you came from—and soon."

Mrs. Nelson thrust a basket of hot rolls into Andi's hands, effectively cutting off any further discussion of the matter. She lifted a heaping platter of fried chicken and nodded toward the door.

Andi reentered the dining room in time to hear Felicity complaining about a horse. She listened with only half an ear as she watched Mrs. Nelson place the plate of chicken on the table and return to the kitchen. Andi followed suit, hoping she, too, could disappear quickly from sight.

"Girl." Randle Livingston's voice stopped Andi in her tracks. "We need our water glasses filled." He nodded toward the pitcher, which sat less than six inches from his empty glass.

Without a word, Andi lifted the heavy pitcher. She made her way around the table filling glasses and wishing she could give into the temptation to "accidentally" spill the entire contents of the pitcher into Felicity's lap. She was smiling at the thought when she reached for Senator Farley's glass.

The senator caught Andi's gaze and held it. A puzzled expression crossed his face. He opened his mouth to say something, then closed it and shook his head. Instead, he took his glass and simply whispered, "Thank you."

Andi ducked her head and moved on.

"I've had it up to here with that new horse," Felicity was grumbling. "I've tried everything I know to make her mind, but nothing's working."

Randle Livingston smiled. "Have you tried making friends with the animal, darling? That has sometimes been known to make a difference."

Felicity pouted. "I tried that already. The mare bit me!"

Good for the mare, Andi declared silently, filling another glass with water.

"Have you ridden the horse much?" the young man at Felicity's right asked politely.

"Ha!" Felicity burst out. "If you can call it that. She lets me mount up. After that, I never know what to expect."

Randle put his fork down and gave his daughter a look of surprise. "You've had her two weeks, Felicity. You should have made progress by this time. Perhaps she's not the right horse for you."

"Oh, she is, Papa! I know she's the one! She has everything I've been looking for in a horse—beauty, strength, spirit." She narrowed her eyes. "Matt says if I just keep up the training, she'll eventually come around."

"Training?" Mr. Livingston snorted. "You mean whipping." He raised a finger toward her. "Remember what I told you, Felicity. You go easy on this horse. You've already ruined two perfectly good horses because of your impatience. There are other ways—"

"But, Papa!" Felicity interrupted. "I want fast results. I want to ride my horse and show her off in front of my friends in town. I won't be thrown again. I won't!"

Her father shrugged and returned to his meal. "I mean what I say, Felicity. I don't want you to come crying to me for a new horse in another month."

Andi gripped the water pitcher tightly to keep her hands from shaking. Her heart squeezed in compassion for the poor horse forced to endure Felicity's cruelty. No horse back home had ever felt the sting of the lash. Any wrangler foolish enough to mistreat a horse on the Circle C Ranch soon found himself out of a job. *I can't bear to listen to this,* she thought. *I have to find a way to help!*

"Girl!" Felicity's father reached out and shook Andi from her day-dreaming. "What's the matter with you? Don't stand there like a simpleton. Finish pouring our water and get back to the kitchen."

Andi finished her task and fled. Mercifully, Mrs. Nelson dismissed her for the evening, and she headed for the small shack she shared with the Garduño family. Although her body was tired, her mind swarmed with plans to rescue Felicity's horse.

Andi sighed. She'd probably get into a heap of trouble, but she couldn't stand by and let Felicity abuse any animal on a whim.

She just couldn't.

Chapter Twelve

A STARTLING DISCOVERY

The next few days passed in a blur. Felicity kept Andi so busy that she couldn't do anything about the unlucky horse in the barn. Neither did she have a free moment to slip away and question the Lazy L ranch hands about Taffy. When she wasn't dusting or sweeping floors, she was emptying chamber pots, polishing Felicity's boots, or fetching a cool glass of lemonade or a shawl for her mistress.

Felicity delighted in assigning Andi numerous menial jobs to remind her she was nothing more than a servant. Worse, the older girl never seemed satisfied with Andi's work. A harsh tongue-lashing greeted her every day. Andi had never been bossed around so much in her entire life.

Late one morning, she lifted the heavy bucket of water she'd used to scrub the kitchen floor and hauled it out the back door. The scent of lilacs and roses greeted her.

Andi took a deep breath and sighed. She almost wished Senator Farley had recognized her at supper the other night. He'd have seen her safely home by now, and perhaps it would have been for the best. Her stay on the Lazy L certainly hadn't brought her any closer to finding Taffy, nor did it seem likely she'd have time this morning to wander around the ranch and question the cowhands. Mrs. Nelson had gone into town with a long list and left Andi, Rosa, and Nila with the unhappy chore of thoroughly scouring the kitchen from floor to ceiling. It would probably take the rest of the day. Nila had been busy since sunrise cleaning out ashes and blacking the huge stove.

Andi tossed the dirty water from the bucket onto the flowerbed that bordered the kitchen porch. She dropped the bucket to the ground and leaned against a post, enjoying the sun on her face. She closed her eyes and let the warmth creep into her tired body.

She was just deciding she could rest a few minutes longer when she heard a tremendous crash. Her eyes flew open. From the barn came more crashing, the high-pitched whinny of a horse in pain, and a loud shrieking.

Rosa came running onto the back porch. "The noise! What is it?" she whispered in a frightened voice.

Andi shook her head. "Something's going on in the barn. I don't know what." She took a step off the porch and waited, her heart pounding at the terror in the horse's cry.

Suddenly, the shrieks became clear words. "Stupid, unmanageable horse!"

Andi recognized the voice at once. It turned her blood to ice. Even from this distance, she could hear the slap of Felicity's riding crop. She clenched her fists as the horse screamed again. Her decision to rescue the animal came back in full force and swept all weariness away.

"Oh, Rosa!" she exclaimed, clutching her friend's arm for support. "Felicity is at it again. I can't stand it. I've got to *do* something."

"No!" Rosa shook her head. "Come away. Forget the horse," she urged, pulling Andi onto the porch. "The *señorita* terrifies me. You must not cross her."

"I have to rescue that horse," Andi said, blinking back tears. "I'll ride him home and ask for help finding Taffy—like I should have done days ago." She set her jaw and jerked her chin toward the barn. "Taffy can wait, but the poor horse in there can't."

Her decision made, Andi snatched up the bucket and hurried into the kitchen. Rosa scurried after her, shaking her head and mumbling her disapproval of Andi's plan.

"I need more rags," Nila said, turning from the stove. "They are in the bin across from—" She frowned. "*¿Qué pasa, hijas?*"

Andi dropped the bucket onto the floor and took a deep breath. "It's time for me to go home, *señora*."

Nila's face broke into a wide smile. She nodded her head in agreement. "*¡Qué bueno!* You have come to your senses at last." She turned to her daughter. "Is that not wonderful news, Rosita?"

Rosa appeared too upset to reply.

Andi crossed over to Nila and lowered her voice. "But I'm going to do a very bad thing, *señora*. I'm going to steal a horse." Before Nila could express her astonishment, Andi went on. "I don't want to do it, but I've *got* to get the horse away from Felicity, at least for a little while."

"Don't let her do it, *Mamá*!" Rosa pleaded, wringing her hands.

Nila trembled and shook her head. "This is a foolish and dangerous idea, Andrea. If you are caught, you will be punished. I do not think the law will care that you are only a child."

Andi nodded. "I know. I'm not going to do it in broad daylight. I'll leave tonight—when everyone's asleep."

Nila sighed her acceptance and drew Andi into a warm hug. "Well then, *chiquita, vaya con Dios*—go with God. May He guide you safely home."

"*Vaya con Dios*," Rosa echoed, sniffing back tears. She threw her arms around Andi. "I will miss you."

"I'll miss you, too." Andi pulled away from her friends and forced a smile. "I'll be right back to help you. I want to see which stall the horse is in so I can find it after dark."

Andi stepped onto the porch and nearly collided with the housekeeper, who was striding purposefully toward the door. "Mrs. Nelson," she stammered, skipping out of the woman's path. "You're back so soon. Did you forget something?"

"I wish to speak with you, Andrea," Mrs. Nelson said sharply. "Immediately."

Andi swallowed her surprise and followed the unsmiling woman into the house. At Rosa's questioning look, Andi shrugged. She had no idea why the housekeeper wanted to see her.

Mrs. Nelson marched through the kitchen, pausing only long enough to remove her hat and shawl before continuing her brisk walk down the hallway. Her heels clicked noisily against the wooden floor. When she reached the library, she stopped and motioned Andi to enter. Then she followed behind and slid the doors shut with a resounding *clunk*.

Silence fell. Andi watched uneasily while Mrs. Nelson unfolded a piece of paper she was clutching in her hand. It grew in size until Andi recognized a Wanted poster similar to others she'd seen hanging in the sheriff's office in Fresno.

Mrs. Nelson thrust the paper toward Andi. "I came across this in town. It might interest you."

Andi took the poster from Mrs. Nelson with a trembling hand. She stared in dismay at the letters screaming at her from across the top of the page: **MISSING!** And under it, more bold lettering: **REWARD: $1,000**. A fair likeness of herself mocked her from below the words. Her eyes blurred when she read her name. "Oh *no!*" she murmured in a choked voice.

"You're Elizabeth Carter's girl," Mrs. Nelson stated bluntly.

Andi nodded, speechless.

The housekeeper snatched the poster from Andi's hand and refolded it. Then she stuffed it into her sleeve. "This is a fine kettle of fish," she scolded. "The Carters are an important family in this part of California. A respected family. You should not be working as a servant to the Livingstons. It's shameful. As of right now, you are dismissed. Pack your things. Someone will drive you to the railroad depot. You're going home."

"But—"

"Do as I say—at once," Mrs. Nelson insisted. "The train leaves in an hour."

Andi bit back her protest and followed the housekeeper out of the library and down the hall. Through eyes blurred by unshed tears, she left the house and started toward the small cabin she shared with the Garduño family. She would change into her overalls and return the skirt and blouse Nila had lent her. *Now I won't get a chance to free the horse,* she moaned silently. *What will happen to it?*

Andi threw a final, sorrowful glance toward the barn and paused in surprise. Felicity was standing in the corral, waving her hands and shouting at a dusty cowhand. Behind her, an obviously upset horse tossed its head and whinnied. The cowhand held tightly to the horse's bridle.

"Well?" Felicity demanded. "Can I ride her or not?"

The young man gave the bridle a vicious jerk and whacked the trembling animal. "Why sure, Miss Felicity. I reckon you can do anything you set your mind to. Just give it another try."

Felicity positioned one foot in the stirrup and glared at the ranch hand. "Don't you dare let go," she ordered, tucking her riding crop under her arm. She reached up and caught the saddle horn, then hoisted herself carefully onto the horse's back. "So far, so good." She nodded at the cowhand. He released the bridle and left the corral to join a group of interested onlookers lounging against the barn.

Fascinated with this scene, Andi rubbed her eyes free of tears and hurried over to the corral. She climbed onto the lowest railing and leaned over the top of the fence. Then she took a good, long look at Felicity's horse.

With a shock that took her breath away, Andi recognized Taffy. She let go of the railing and staggered backward, shaking her head in disbelief. *It can't be!* she screamed inwardly. It would be better if Taffy were lost forever than to be here, mistreated and frightened. *It's another palomino,* she reasoned. *It must be.*

Sick to her stomach, but realizing she had to discover the truth, Andi crept back to the fence. She peered between the railings at the horse and rider. Felicity was trotting around the corral, waving her whip and laughing shrilly.

"I knew I'd break her!" she rejoiced. "Look at me, Matt! I—"

Without warning, the palomino stopped short. Felicity flew over her head and landed on the ground like a sack of feed. She groaned.

Andi clapped a hand over her mouth to smother her astonishment. Her gaze swept over the horse. Her heart squeezed. It *was* Taffy. Her four white socks, the white stripe down her nose, the creamy mane and tail—she easily recognized them up close. She didn't even need to see the brand mark to know she'd found her horse.

She watched Taffy trot away from the moaning figure lying in the dust. "Good for you, Taffy," she whispered from behind the fence.

Felicity rose shakily to her feet. She hurried after Taffy and snatched up the reins. With her free hand, she brought the riding crop down across the mare's neck. "I'll teach you not to throw me."

Taffy shuddered and tossed her head, snorting her fear and anger. She tried to shy away from the stinging blows, but Felicity held her fast.

With a cry of outrage, Andi leaped into action. She threw open the corral gate and raced across the enclosure, planting herself between Felicity and Taffy. "Don't you *dare* hit this horse!" she commanded, shaking in anger. She clenched her fists to keep them still.

Felicity's face showed her surprise. "What business is it of yours? She's my horse. I'll do as I please with her. As for you . . ." Her eyes narrowed. "What are you doing out here? Get back to work."

Andi ignored her. She reached out to Taffy and threw her arms around her neck, burying her face in the mare's creamy mane. Taffy immediately settled down. She nuzzled Andi's shoulder and nickered softly.

"Oh, Taffy," Andi murmured into the mare's ear. "I found you."

A sudden crack like a bee sting caught Andi across her shoulders. She yelped and whirled around.

"Get your filthy hands off my horse," Felicity ordered sharply. She raised her whip to emphasize her command.

Blazing with anger, Andi flew at Felicity. She yanked the whip from her hand and clutched it tightly. She looked at her golden horse, crisscrossed with thin, red cuts. Then she turned and glared at Felicity. "I'd like to give you a good dose of what you gave my horse," she said, struggling to hold back her fury. "But"—she flung the whip away from her in disgust—"that would be wrong."

"*Your* horse?" A dark flush crept up Felicity's neck and into her face. "Get out of here, you impudent girl!"

Andi reached out and caught hold of Taffy's bridle. "Don't worry. We're leaving." She stroked Taffy's nose and whispered, "It's all over now. I won't let her hurt you again."

"The horse stays," Felicity said. "My father bought her. If you take her, you'll be stealing." She drew a deep, shaky breath. "I'm warning you . . ."

Andi turned her back on Felicity and mounted Taffy in one smooth motion. Sitting astride her horse, she felt at peace for the first time since leaving home. She was glad she didn't have to steal an unknown horse to save it from Felicity's abuse. Taking back her own mare didn't bother her conscience a bit. She felt only a weary sense of relief that she could go back to her family at last, ask forgiveness, and accept the punishment she knew she deserved. "Come on, Taffy," she said. "Let's get out of here."

Taffy leaped into a canter, clearly as anxious as Andi to be free of the Lazy L. They flew through the open gate of the corral and down the broad lane leading to the road.

"Come back here!" Felicity shrieked.

Andi glanced back to see Felicity running around, ordering the men to give chase. Three of the hired hands mounted up and galloped after her. Andi grinned. She knew Taffy could easily outrun those cow ponies. The thrill of a race surged through her. "Go, Taffy!" she shouted in delight.

Taffy broke into a gallop.

Less than a minute later, Andi's joy turned to dismay. A group of men were riding up the driveway toward her. *Oh, no!* She moaned. *They must be more Lazy L hands.*

"Stop her!" Felicity's voice was faint but clear. "She's stealing my horse!"

The men went into action. They spread themselves out across the wide lane, blocking Taffy's forward movement. Trapped on either side by hundreds of yards of white fencing, Andi realized she had little choice but to stop. To jump the fence on such short notice was too risky. She slowed Taffy to a walk and allowed the hands to escort her back to the ranch.

When Andi returned to the corral, Felicity was waiting for her. Her eyes glinted dangerously, and her lips twisted into a sneer. Without a word, she seized Taffy's bridle and yanked the horse to an abrupt halt.

Andi swallowed in sudden fear. Maybe—just maybe—she should have hazarded the jump, after all.

Chapter Thirteen

TRAPPED!

G et off my horse and off my father's ranch, you miserable thief,"
Felicity ordered, grasping Andi by the arm. "I never want to
see you again." She dragged her from the saddle and gave her a rough
shove, which sent Andi tumbling to the ground.

It was a bad mistake. Taffy snorted, sidestepped, then stretched
out her neck and nipped Felicity on the arm.

"She bit me!" Felicity yelped and jumped back, rubbing her arm.
"She'll pay for that." She reached down and scooped up her riding
crop. "I'll teach this horse a lesson she won't soon forget."

Andi felt the blood drain from her face. Fear for Taffy replaced her
anger at Felicity. She glanced wildly around the yard, searching for
an adult—*any* adult who would keep Felicity from carrying out her
plans. Her gaze fell on the small group of ranch hands beside the
barn. With her heart in her throat, she darted across the corral. "Oh,
please!" she shouted, throwing herself to the top of the railing. "You've
got to stop her. Taffy's too good a horse to be whipped. Felicity will
ruin her."

One of the men shook his head. It was obvious he wanted no part
of this. He walked away and disappeared behind the barn. Three
others followed.

"The only orders that count on this ranch come from the boss or
Miss Felicity," a tall, lanky cowhand remarked, pushing back his hat.
He shrugged. "It's her horse. Besides, a lick or two never hurt no
horse—especially a stubborn one." He folded his arms across his chest

and spit a stream of tobacco juice in Andi's direction. Then he saun-tered off to the bunkhouse.

Andi dropped from the railing and raced back to Felicity. Her heart pounded against her chest like a hammer. She snatched at the riding crop, but Felicity was faster.

"Get out of my way," Felicity ordered, holding the whip over her head, out of Andi's reach.

Andi looked up into the older girl's face and clenched her fists. "You're a wicked, wicked girl to whip a good horse just because you can't manage her any other way."

A sudden, painful tightening around her arm told Andi her com-ment had struck home. "I've taken as much as I'm going to take from the likes of you," Felicity hissed. "And this horse is never going to bite me again!"

"You deserve to be bitten," Andi shot back. She shook free from Felicity's grip and threw her arms around Taffy's neck. "I won't let you touch her."

"We'll see about that," Felicity declared, taking a step away from the pair. She shook her head. "You should never have tried to steal my horse."

"I didn't steal your horse," Andi insisted. "Look at the brand! Circle C. She's a Carter horse, and I'm Andrea Carter."

"Ha! You're nothing but a servant girl and a thief." Felicity raised her whip. "Now, step aside."

Andi clung to Taffy and tried to think. What could she say to change Felicity's mind? "Please, Felicity," she pleaded, her throat so tight she could hardly speak. "Don't hit her. I'll show you how to handle her. I'll help you—"

"*You?* Help *me?*" Felicity's laugh was a loud bark. "Never! This horse will learn things *my* way. Now . . . get away from my horse."

Andi gulped back her fear and shook her head. "No. You won't whip Taffy. Not ever."

In an instant, Felicity sprang. She yanked Andi away from Taffy and shoved her to the ground.

Andi lay still and tried to catch her breath. She shook her head to clear it. Any moment, she expected to hear the whistling of the whip and her horse's terrified whinnies. When nothing happened, she glanced up. Felicity towered over her, the riding crop poised to strike.

"Felicity! No!" Andi shouted in sudden, awful understanding. Had Felicity lost her mind? She scrambled to her feet.

The first stroke of Felicity's riding whip across her back sent Andi to the ground with a gasp. A wave of pain and humiliation washed over her. She heard Felicity's low-throated chuckle and tried to rise. Before she could scurry away, the second blow fell. Andi clenched her jaw to keep from crying out.

"This will put you in your place, thief," Felicity murmured, striking her a third time, then a fourth. "Then I'll deal with my horse."

"She's . . . not . . . your . . . horse." Andi forced the words out between breaths. Desperately, she threw herself beneath Taffy's belly in an attempt to avoid Felicity's quick, stinging blows. She crawled to the other side of her horse and stood up, clutching Taffy's creamy mane for support. She blinked back tears of pain. *She can't make me cry!* she told herself, taking a deep breath.

Felicity appeared at Taffy's rear. She raised her crop and brought it down with a loud *whack* against the mare's rump. Taffy screamed and bolted, sending Andi to the ground in a crumpled heap.

"Felicity!" Randle Livingston's voice sliced the air like a knife. Andi looked up. Felicity's father approached the corral in long, angry strides, followed by an obviously distraught Mrs. Nelson. With a mighty shove, he threw open the gate and stalked over to his daughter. "Have you taken leave of your senses?" he demanded, tearing the whip from Felicity's hand. He glanced down at Andi with a worried frown. "Are you all right?"

"I feel sick," Andi whispered, swallowing hard. She made no move to get up, but bowed her head and tried to keep her churning stomach from disgracing her. Her throat was tight and her eyes burned with unshed tears.

"See to the girl," Randle instructed Mrs. Nelson. Then he turned back to Felicity. "I thought I made it clear this was not to happen again."

"It was an accident, Papa," Felicity explained in a small voice. "The horse bit me." She rubbed her arm. "I was disciplining the mare, and the girl got in the way. That's all."

"That's *all*?" her father asked, piercing his daughter with his dark gaze.

Felicity shrugged. "She stole my horse. Just mounted her and rode off. I couldn't let her do that, could I?"

Randle frowned. He turned to Andi, who was leaning her head against Mrs. Nelson's shoulder. "Why would you steal Felicity's horse?"

"She's not Felicity's horse," Andi explained. "She's mine."

"That's ridiculous. And an outright lie," Felicity insisted.

"Sir," Mrs. Nelson interrupted, glancing up from Andi's side. "This child needs tending. It looks like she took a pretty good whipping before you got here."

Randle gave Andi a quick glance. "She looks all right, Agatha. Don't concern yourself. Just send her back to her cabin for the rest of the day. She'll be fine by tomorrow morning."

Mrs. Nelson helped Andi to her feet and fixed an unyielding gaze on her employer. "It would be much wiser to settle this girl in the guest room and ask Dr. Tanner to take a look at her injuries." She reached into her sleeve and withdrew the notice that Andi had seen only a short time ago. "You'd better take a look at this."

Randle gave his housekeeper a puzzled look and took the paper from her hand. There was silence while his eyes scanned the page, then he let out a long, deep sigh and looked at Andi. "I don't think Doc Tanner's services are required," he said, returning his gaze to the poster. "The fewer people who know about this, the better." He glanced at Felicity, who had become very quiet. "I have my daughter's reputation to consider. Her emotions are fragile. I won't have her upset."

Mrs. Nelson drew herself up to her full height and faced the huge man. "It's not a peasant child stealing a handkerchief this time," she reminded him. "You won't be able to cover it up so easily. When the Carters learn—"

"You forget yourself, Agatha." Randle's voice crackled with annoyance.

The woman held her employer's gaze. "Of course, sir," she replied stiffly. "Forgive me."

He nodded. "Do what you think best for the girl's injuries, but leave that money-grubbing Doc Tanner out of this." He tapped the poster with his finger and grunted. "He'd wire Fresno quicker than you can say 'reward.'" He crumpled the poster into a ball and crammed it into his pocket.

𝐂

Andi sat on the window seat of the Livingstons' elegant guest room, staring outside. Through the glass, she could see her beautiful, golden palomino mare standing patiently in the corral. Taffy shook her head, and her creamy mane flew out in all directions. She flicked her ears forward in an attitude of anticipation, as if she expected her true mistress to return at any moment.

Andi watched until two ranch hands entered the corral and led the mare toward the barn. Taffy did not go willingly. She reared up and flailed her legs in protest. Andi clenched her fists at the sight, helpless to do anything about it. She turned from the window in despair. A lump grew in her throat until she couldn't swallow, and she blinked furiously to keep her tears in check.

"Andrea?" Nila's kind voice echoed softly in the room.

Andi looked up. Her Mexican friend carried a basin and towel, which she set on a small table. She crossed to the window seat and sat down. Placing one of Andi's small hands in her own, she gave it a gentle squeeze. "I am so sorry, *chiquita*. I wish we had never come to this *rancho*."

Andi drew a deep, shaky breath and shook her head. "Don't say that," she protested. "After all, I found my horse." She glanced back toward the window, but Taffy had disappeared.

"True. But at what price?"

Andi bowed her head. "It hurts, *señora*. It feels like a thousand bees are stinging my back, and—and—I want my mother."

"Of course you do." Nila pulled her into a gentle embrace, mindful of her injured back. "Now, come lie on the bed while I tend your injuries."

Andi made her way over to the huge, four-poster bed and climbed up. She lay down on her stomach and buried her head in the feather pillow. She squeezed her eyes shut and waited.

Nila gently lifted the back of Andi's blouse and clicked her tongue in concern. "This may sting a little," she warned, reaching for the basin. With gentle hands, she began to gently probe and clean the worst of the welts.

"Are you almost finished?" Andi asked a few minutes later, digging her fingers into the pillow.

"*Sí.*" Nila replied. "I am applying the salve now."

Andi shuddered when the cold mixture touched her bare skin. Then she felt her blouse being lowered. She sat up. "*Gracias, señora.*"

Nila nodded and began to gather up the towels and medicine.

Suddenly, without any warning or the courtesy of a knock, the door flew open. Randle Livingston entered the room. "So, how's the patient?"

"It's not polite to enter a room without knocking," Andi retorted, scowling.

Randle chuckled and settled himself at the foot of the bed. "You're certainly full of sass today." He nodded, clearly pleased. "That's good. It means you're not seriously hurt—except maybe for your pride. Felicity told me the whole story, and I believe it was nothing more than a misunderstanding between you girls."

Andi frowned in confusion. "What do you mean, Mr. Livingston?"

"You made a mistake. Felicity reacted poorly. A few days of rest—maybe a week or two—and you'll agree this incident was just a silly quarrel not worth remembering."

"A week or two?" Andi stared at the man in disbelief. "I'm going home *today*, Mrs. Nelson said so. Now that I've found my horse I—"

Randle was shaking his head. "I'm afraid not, Miss Carter. I can't allow you to return to your family in your present condition. Your mother might read more into this small incident than I'd like. She could make my life difficult. For Felicity's sake, you will stay here until you are completely healed from your . . . *accident*. Then it will be only your word against mine."

"What about my horse?"

"That's between you and Felicity. But . . ." Randle caught Andi's gaze and held it. "I recommend you give up the horse—for your own sake." He stood up and crossed the room. When he reached the door, he paused. "One more thing, Miss Carter. Consider yourself my guest for the next several days. This is your room. Please don't leave it. As long as you honor my request and behave like a guest, I will treat you as one. Do anything that brings shame to Felicity, and you will pay the price."

Andi gulped back her dismay at the man's words. She was trapped, but good.

Chapter Fourteen

FELICITY'S PLAN

A s soon as Randle Livingston closed the guest room door, Andi burst into tears. She threw herself onto the bed and buried her head in the pillow, sobbing her heart out. Two more weeks! She couldn't bear to be away from home for two more weeks, now that she'd found Taffy.

Nila grasped her by the shoulders and began hushing her in quiet tones. Andi relaxed and rolled over to face her friend, wincing when the bedcovers rubbed against her sore back.

"The *patrón* said something that upset you," Nila said quietly.

Andi nodded and sat up. "He won't let me go home, *señora*. He's afraid. He wants to keep Felicity from taking any blame for what she did to me. He can't see how cruel and selfish she really is." Andi shook her head. "Worst of all, he won't give me my horse." Fresh tears threatened to spill over. She rubbed her eyes furiously. Crying did no good. It didn't even make her feel better—only worse.

"*¡Qué lástima!*" Nila clucked in sympathy. "What a pity!"

Andi bit her lip and tried to think. Would Mr. Livingston keep her locked in her room? Even if he didn't and she somehow managed to sneak out of the house, how would she leave the ranch? Steal another horse? No, she decided. That hadn't worked well the first time. There were too many people lingering around the yard to escape unnoticed. She paused. Perhaps there was another way.

"*Señora,*" she said, "I need your help. You've got to send a wire—a telegram—to the Circle C Ranch, near Fresno. I'll write it out, and the *señor* can go to town and send it. My family will come for me. I know they will."

Nila stared at Andi. Her face lost all color. She clasped her hands together and shook her head. "Please, *chiquita*. Do not ask this of us."

"Why not?" Andi asked in surprise. "It's easy. Take Rosa. She knows enough English to send a telegram."

"It's not that." Nila rose and began pacing the room. "You don't understand. The *patrón* knows you are not one of us. José is afraid the law will come for him because we kept you with us."

"But I'll explain. No one would blame you."

Nila wrung her hands. "Your word will mean nothing if the *patrón* decides to cause trouble for us. He is a rich, important *gringo*."

Andi gazed into the woman's dark, frightened eyes. "You're really afraid, aren't you?"

Nila nodded. "We are strangers in a country we know nothing about, wanting only to be left alone to live in peace. You have been much help to us over the past few weeks, and we are grateful. However, I'm afraid José will not agree to send a telegram. I am so sorry, *chiquita*."

Andi watched Nila's eyes brim with tears. She knew her friend was torn up inside at her decision. "*Está bien, señora*," she assured her, even though it really wasn't all right at all. "I'll think of something else."

Nila nodded her thanks and scooped up the basin and towels. "I must get back to work," she said. "Perhaps the *señora* will allow me to return later in the day. *Adiós, chiquita*."

But Nila did not come back.

It was Mrs. Nelson, looking grimmer than ever, who brought Andi her supper tray—and news of the Garduño family. "They're gone," she explained in answer to Andi's question. "Mr. Livingston dismissed them himself—along with a few parting words of advice."

What the advice was, Mrs. Nelson would not say. But Andi could guess, and it chilled her to the bone. She opened her mouth to plead with the woman to help her, but a new voice broke in.

"Good heavens, Agatha!" Felicity exclaimed, hurrying into the guest room. She was carrying a small lap desk and clutched it tightly to her chest. "So now you're bringing this . . . this . . . housemaid a supper tray?" She came and stood beside the bed, scowling at Mrs. Nelson.

Mrs. Nelson regarded Felicity silently for a moment. Then she spoke. "I have work to do, Miss, so if you'll excuse me?" She turned and left.

Felicity ignored the disapproval in the housekeeper's voice. Her gaze darted around the room before coming to rest on Andi. "I see Papa has decided to treat you like a guest rather than the servant you are." She jerked her chin toward the tray. "Your supper's getting cold."

Andi didn't care. She'd lost her appetite the minute Felicity appeared in the doorway.

"Meals in your room. Leisure time." Felicity smirked. "All you lack now are decent clothes to replace those peasant rags you're wearing."

Andi bristled at the mocking tone but held her tongue.

Felicity settled herself into a large, overstuffed chair in the corner of the room. She pulled her lap desk onto her knees and opened it. From inside, she took out a piece of paper. She spoke, and the change in her voice put Andi instantly on guard. "I've been thinking all afternoon, Andrea," she said pleasantly. "Perhaps we could avoid a misunderstanding if I were to draw up a little agreement between us."

"What sort of agreement?" Andi asked.

Felicity brought the paper over to the bed and dropped it in Andi's lap. She shrugged. "It's a bill of sale. Quite ordinary."

Andi frowned. "A bill of sale for what?"

"You know perfectly well what it's for," Felicity snapped, eyes blazing. She looked ready to strike. Then she smiled, took a deep breath, and composed herself. "There's going to be trouble over that silly horse. We can't both have her. Even if she did belong to you at one time, she's mine now. I want you to sign this bill of sale to make it all nice and legal. In return"—she fished around in a small purse hanging from her wrist and brought out two shiny gold coins—"I'm prepared to pay you twenty dollars, as a token of my goodwill."

Andi gaped at Felicity. She was so astonished at the girl's outrageous attempt to keep Taffy that she didn't know what to say. Slowly, she picked up the paper and scanned it. *It looks like a real bill of sale. Just like the ones I've seen Justin fill out.* There was a detailed description of Taffy, her previous owner, new owner, price paid, date   even the brand mark. Near the bottom of the page a long, black, dotted line shouted for a signature.

"Well?" Felicity pressed.

Andi held the bill of sale at arm's length. "Here's what I think of your offer," she declared, ripping the paper in two. "You're crazy to think I'd sell you *any* horse—much less my best friend." She let the two halves flutter to the floor. "Now, go away and leave me alone."

Felicity's face turned a dull red. She bent down to pick up the torn bill of sale. "You'll be sorry you did that," she hissed, stuffing the papers into her lap desk. "Very sorry." She left the room, slamming the door with such force it shook the walls.

Squeak. The noise jerked Andi from a troubled sleep. She opened her eyes and looked around. It wasn't quite dawn, judging by the amount of light trickling through the lace curtains of the guest room. What had awakened her? She listened. All was still.

Hearing nothing, she snuggled deeper under the warm quilts, wishing she could fall asleep and wake up in her own bed. "How many times have I wished *that* these past couple of weeks?" she mumbled bitterly. She winced as she tried to find a comfortable position. The sharp, stinging pain from yesterday's encounter with Felicity had dulled to a steady ache. As long as she lay still and made no quick movements, it was bearable.

Andi yawned and pulled the quilt closer around her shoulders. *Go to sleep,* she commanded her whirling thoughts. *Don't think about anything but—*

Without warning, an icy hand clamped down over her mouth. She screamed, but it came out a muffled yelp. Her heart raced. She struggled to sit up.

"Hush!" came a whispered command. "Do you want to wake the entire household?"

Andi stopped struggling. Her pounding heart returned to normal. She reached up and pried Felicity's fingers from her face. "What are you doing?" she demanded in a harsh whisper.

Felicity released her and stepped back. Quickly, she lit the lamp on the bedside table. "It's the mare," she explained, adjusting the flame to a dim yellow glow. "I think she's in bad shape. She won't let Matt or me near her, but she might let you approach."

"*Taffy?*" Andi threw back the quilts and leaped from her bed. She raced for the door.

Felicity snatched her back. "You can't go out in your nightgown. Get dressed. Hurry."

Andi yanked the fine, white cotton nightgown over her head and tossed it to the floor. She shivered in the chilly, predawn air and pulled on the blouse and skirt that Nila had given her. Then she slipped on her boots and stumbled for the door.

"Come quietly," Felicity warned her. "Papa's a light sleeper. Remember, you're not supposed to be out of your room."

Andi gave a hurried nod and let Felicity go first. The older girl, dressed in a riding skirt and warm jacket, led Andi down the stairs and through the kitchen. Placing a finger to her lips, she cracked open the back door and motioned Andi out into the cool, fresh new day.

Andi wasted no time wondering why Felicity was up so early this morning. All her thoughts were focused on Taffy. "What're her symptoms?" she asked, sprinting toward the barn. "Is it colic? Has she gotten into the grain?" She forced the questions out between breaths. "Can she stand?"

Felicity shook her head and kept running. She raced ahead of Andi and disappeared into the barn.

When Andi reached the barn, she was panting from her run and from her fear for Taffy. What could she do? She knew next to nothing about treating sick horses. That was Chad's job—and he did it well. If only he were here now! *If Taffy sickens and dies, it'll be all my fault! Oh, please, God! Don't let her die.*

Felicity's voice called out from the dimly lit barn. "In here!"

Andi hurried inside, calling Taffy's name. She heard an answering whinny and caught a glimpse of a healthy, alert golden palomino before something rough and smelly was thrown over her head. Then everything went dark.

Chapter Fifteen

GOOD-BYE, TAFFY

It took Andi only a few breaths to realize she'd been tricked. Horribly tricked! She was so angry, frightened, and humiliated, she wanted to scream and kick. She could do neither. Strong arms—not Felicity's—wrapped the burlap sack tightly around her body and lifted her into a wagon.

"Felicity!" she managed to gasp, struggling for air.

There was no answer, only a pair of firm hands keeping her flat against the wagon bed. She tried to wriggle free, but her back exploded in pain from the movement. She bit her lip and lay still.

Finally, Felicity whispered, "Hurry, Matt. Let's get moving."

When the rattling and jostling of the wagon finally ceased, Andi could tell through the rough weave of the burlap that the sky had begun to lighten. She didn't resist when Matt hauled her roughly from the wagon and slung her over his shoulder. A set of keys jangled briefly, a door creaked open, and Andi fell to the ground with a groan. Rough hands yanked at the burlap sack, and in a moment she was free.

With one quick glance, Andi took in her surroundings. She found herself sitting on a dirt floor in an old, deserted storage shed—no larger than her horse's stall back home. It was stoutly built of strong, rough-hewn logs. The only light, a pale slice of the early morning sky, came from about seven feet up, through narrow gaps under the roof. A sturdy door, hanging from large, rusting hinges, discouraged thieves from breaking in and stealing whatever had once been stored here. A few pieces of aged, broken farm equipment hung from wooden pegs protruding from the walls, and a pile of tattered feed sacks—thoroughly chewed by rodents—lay in a heap in one corner. It was apparent that no one had used this shed for years.

"What do you think of my little hideaway?" Felicity asked with a smile. "I found it a few years ago—hidden in this little gully away from everything." She shrugged. "The remains of an old cabin are close by. I'd guess it's at least thirty years old. It most likely belonged to some old prospector who never struck it rich and decided to try his hand at farming instead."

"Why, Felicity?" Andi asked, ignoring the history lesson. "Why did you trick me?"

Felicity sighed. "I couldn't very well kidnap you from your room in broad daylight. Too many prying eyes. But I knew exactly how to get you to the barn without a struggle, at a time when no one would be up. Matt was more than willing to help me." She glanced at the tall, lanky cowboy and smiled. "He's sweet on me." Matt grinned back.

"I don't understand any of this," Andi said. "What am I doing here?"

Felicity lost her smile. "I knew you'd never sign the bill of sale as long as you stayed comfortable in my father's guest room." She spread her arms to indicate the shed. "On the other hand, this *new* room will help you decide much more quickly to do as I say. I told you yesterday you'd be sorry. Are you sorry yet?"

Andi felt herself pale. "Not as sorry as *you're* going to be. Your father will raise the roof when he finds out I've disappeared."

Felicity snorted her opinion of that. "Oh, he'll fuss and fume a few days, but he'll never suspect I had anything to do with it. Why should he? And once I get my horse, I won't care what Papa thinks." She dusted off her skirt and pulled a piece of paper from her jacket pocket. "Now, down to business."

Andi sighed wearily. "I'm not signing it. If you try to make me, I'll just tear it up again."

Felicity continued as if Andi hadn't spoken. "When you sign it, I'll let you leave this shed. Until then"—she glanced around—"consider yourself at home."

"You're crazy, Felicity. Completely *loco*. It doesn't make sense to go to all this trouble to own a horse you can't even ride."

"Perhaps you're right," the girl admitted, glancing at the bill of sale. "But it's no longer just a question of ownership."

"It's not?" Andi frowned. She must be tired. She had no idea what Felicity was talking about.

Felicity shook her head. "No. It's the fact that no housemaid—no matter what your name is—will get the best of me." She took a deep breath. "The horse is mine, and your signature on this bill of sale will prove it. Sign it now and you'll save yourself a lot of trouble."

"No."

"Suit yourself," Felicity said. "You'll sign it sooner or later." She stood in the open doorway for a moment, regarding her prisoner. "I'll be back this afternoon to see if you've changed your mind. Here's breakfast." She took a canteen and a small gunnysack from Matt and tossed them at Andi's feet. "Be thinking about how long you'd like to stay in here."

"I'll never sign it," Andi declared in a tight voice. "*Never.*"

"Yes, you will." Felicity closed the door with a loud *thud*. The shed was immediately cast into darkness.

Andi caught her breath and backed into a corner, all courage and brave words forgotten as true, gut-wrenching fear overwhelmed her. "You talk real big, Andi Carter," she muttered to herself, pulling her knees up against her chest to keep from shaking. "But that's all it is— *talk*." She buried her head in her arms and let the tears come.

Andi heard the key turn in the lock and stood up. She braced herself for another confrontation with Felicity. For two full days and nights she had sat in this filthy shed and waited and waited and . . .

Stop it! she scolded herself. She quickly wiped her eyes so Felicity could not see that she'd been crying again. There wasn't much to do in this dismal place but cry and pray, and Andi had been doing plenty of both.

She'd poured out her heart to God during those long, lonely hours when she was certain she would die of fear. She knew He'd heard her and even forgiven her for the foolish and wrong things she'd done lately, but it came as a pleasant surprise to actually feel less afraid after she prayed. The peace of knowing that God still loved her and was with her even in this dreary shed was a gift she wasn't about to forget.

Oh, Lord, she prayed as the door creaked open, *Help me to be strong and make the right decision for once. I've made too many bad ones lately. What should I do about Taffy?*

Bright sunlight fell into the shed, forcing Andi to blink and cover her eyes. Felicity entered, followed as usual by Matt.

"Ya know, Miss Felicity," Matt was grumbling, "I'm gettin' second thoughts. The boss ain't been too happy the past couple of days, thinkin' the girl's run off an' all. Now, with her family nosin' around, I—"

"Oh, hush, Matt!" Felicity snapped. "You just keep thinking about all those waltzes I'm giving you next week at the spring dance." She reached into her sleeve and pulled out a perfumed handkerchief. Waving the small square of white in front of her nose, she approached Andi and coughed delicately. "Phew! How do you stand the smell in here? Another day of this and you won't be able to breathe." With her other hand, Felicity tossed another sack and canteen at Andi's feet.

Andi made no move to pick them up. She folded her arms across her chest and silently regarded Felicity. She couldn't help noticing how fresh and clean the older girl appeared in her split-skirt, vest, and bright blue blouse. A matching blue bow pulled back her curls.

In contrast, Andi knew she was filthy. The white blouse and color-ful skirt Nila had exchanged so many days ago for her overalls were gray with grime from living on the dirt floor. She had tried to keep her hands and face clean, but the water from the canteen had served only to turn the dust on her hands to mud. Now, in the light of a bright afternoon, she realized just how awful she must look.

Felicity smiled, as if reading Andi's mind. She held up the smudged, wrinkled bill of sale. "Ready to get out of here? Don't you want to go home?"

Home! Andi stared at the paper. *Yes, I want to go home, but . . .*

"What good does this do?" Matt complained from the doorway. He leaned against the doorpost and crossed his long, gangly arms over his chest. "She won't change her mind."

"She will today," Felicity replied without turning around. "Won't you, Andrea?"

Andi looked past Felicity into the freedom of a lovely afternoon. *Home!* It would be so easy to sign the paper and walk away from this place. Then she remembered the lash marks on her horse. She shook her head. She couldn't leave Taffy with Felicity.

A sly smile curled Felicity's lips. "I met your family today."

The words struck Andi like a slap in the face. She flinched. "You're lying."

"You don't believe me? It's one of the reasons I'm late coming to see you." She settled herself near the open doorway and stared at the ceiling as if deep in thought. "Let's see if I remember this right. Your mother has light hair, with just a little gray. She dresses nicely and carries herself like a lady. Your sister is golden-haired and real pretty. About my age, wouldn't you say?"

Andi found herself holding her breath at Felicity's words. Her mind was spinning. Her family was here? On the Lazy L? It was incredible. How . . . ?

Felicity was still talking. "I wouldn't mind getting to know your brothers better. They're quite good-looking." She blushed. "The two older ones are dark-haired—like you, but the younger brother is blond and so very friendly."

"He won't be so friendly when he finds out what you did to me," Andi replied. From Felicity's descriptions, she knew the girl spoke the truth about her family's arrival on the ranch. "How did they find me?"

"They *haven't* found you," Felicity reminded Andi with a laugh. "They're up at the house. You're tucked away here, where they'll never find you." She rose to her feet and brushed the dust from her skirt. "They'll be leaving soon. Papa told them he didn't know where you were—which is the truth. I guess they'll look around a bit, ask folks in town, and head back to their fancy ranch up north." She sighed. "A pity, really. Your mother looked so tired and sad."

A lump came to Andi's throat. Her mother was here, looking for her. Her brothers—and even Melinda—had come, hoping to find her on the Lazy L. They must be very worried. She'd been gone so long.

I'm getting out of here, she decided, swallowing hard. The lump in her throat disappeared. *My family's not going home without me! They've suffered enough on my account.*

Andi squared her shoulders and looked at the paper in Felicity's hand. She realized she was not going to win this battle. Suddenly, it didn't matter so much if she won. What really mattered was going home. It was the right decision—the only decision. She had to give Taffy up.

"I'll sign it," she said, clenching her jaw. With an ache in her heart that hurt worse than Felicity's whip, she held out her hand. Smiling in triumph, Felicity took a filled pen from her pocket and thrust the paper under Andi's nose.

Andi scrawled her name on the dotted line. Just like that, she condemned her best friend to the likes of Felicity Livingston. She choked back a sob and threw the pen and paper to the ground.

Felicity smiled and snatched up her precious document. "You're free to go. I don't care where. But don't *ever* step foot on the Lazy L again." She pointed toward the faint outline of a little-used road leading west. "Town is that way. Start walking."

Andi brushed past Felicity.

"Oh, I almost forgot," Felicity called her back. She grabbed Andi's hand and slapped two shiny gold coins in her palm. "Here's your twenty dollars—just to keep things legal."

Andi flung the money at Felicity's feet. Then she turned and fled.

Chapter Sixteen

A LONG WALK

Andi didn't know how far it was to town or what she would do when she got there. She only knew she was hot, sweaty, and dreadfully tired. She hoped she wasn't lost. The old wagon path Felicity had pointed out wound its way alongside gullies and through small creeks for what seemed like an eternity. When it finally joined up with a road that looked well traveled, Andi stopped to rest. A crooked sign with the words *Livingston Flats—3 mi.* and an arrow pointed the way to town.

"Three more miles!" Andi exclaimed, dismayed. She shook her head, took a deep breath, and slowly began the trek into town. As she trudged along the dusty road, she thought about what would happen when she reached Livingston Flats. Perhaps the sheriff would let her stay in his office. Maybe he'd get her something to eat. She shook her head and looked down at herself. *Most likely he'll toss me into the horse trough first.*

She sighed. Worse than seeing the sheriff was the thought of explaining Taffy's new owner to her family. Never had she dreamed it would end like this. How foolish she had been! She should have returned home the minute the Garduño family offered to take her. She should have let her brothers find her horse, instead of insisting on the hopeless task of searching for Taffy on her own. She'd done everything wrong. Again. Even knowing she was forgiven didn't ease the bitterness of leaving Taffy behind.

The minutes crawled by. Andi shaded her eyes, longing to see some sign of civilization. The town appeared as a smudge of dark shapes on the horizon. *This is the longest three miles of my life,* she decided. Spotting a huge oak tree next to the road, she headed for it, threw herself to the ground beneath its spreading branches, and let out a grateful sigh. What a relief to be out from under the glaring sun! She leaned against the trunk of the ancient hardwood and gazed down the seemingly endless road.

"If only a rider would come by. Or a wagon, or a . . . well, anything with wheels or hooves. I wouldn't be too proud to ask for a ride." She saw no one. Her eyelids began to flutter. "I'll just close my eyes for one minute," she murmured.

The sound of hoofbeats roused Andi from her dozing. She yawned and blinked against the brightness of the afternoon. A horse and rider were galloping toward her from the direction of the Livingston ranch. She jumped up, suddenly alert.

Andi cupped her hands to her mouth and shouted at the top of her lungs. "Hey, you! Whoever you are! Stop!" In her excitement at discovering a potential ride, she completely forgot no one could possibly hear her from so far away. She waved her arms wildly over her head and took off running down the road, hoping to attract the rider's attention.

It worked. The rider yanked back on the reins when Andi planted herself in the animal's path. "Whoa, there!" he barked. The horse came to an abrupt standstill, churning up a cloud of dust with his stamping hooves.

Andi, out of breath and desperate for a ride, stumbled against the horse. He shied away, but she reached out and grasped the bridle. "Please, mister," she pleaded, coughing hard from the choking dust. "I need a ride." She looked up into the rider's face. "Are you headed for—" She broke off with a gasp. "Chad!"

Chad's mouth fell open. "*Andi?*" With a slight pull on the reins, he steadied his horse and leaped from the saddle. "Are you all right? Where've you been?"

Andi hesitated only a moment. Then she launched herself at her brother and threw her arms around his neck, nearly choking him in her embrace. "Oh, Chad!" she said, gulping back tears. "You're here! You found me! How? How did you know where to look?"

"Hey! Take it easy." Chad laughed. He untangled her shaking arms from around his neck and lowered her to the ground. "It was Senator Farley." Chad nodded at Andi's astonishment. "The senator was passing though town on his way back to Sacramento and learned you were still missing. He told Justin he'd seen a girl on Randle Livingston's ranch he at first thought was you, but then he figured he had to be mistaken when she spoke only Spanish. It was a long shot, but we'd searched everywhere else, so we decided to try the Lazy L." Chad caught her up and gave her another hug. "Some folks might say that's a remarkable coincidence, but I prefer to believe it was the grace of God arranging things."

Andi nodded and slid to the ground. She suddenly felt ashamed—ashamed that her brother looked so happy to see her. He should be angry, disgusted with her behavior. "I'm sorry I ran off," she apologized quietly. "I would've come home that very night, except Taffy got stolen and I had to find her. It's all my fault, and I promise I'll never—"

Chad held up his hand to stop the flow of words. "It's not entirely your fault. I'm to blame for some of it. Me and my big mouth." He let out a long, tired sigh. "But thank God, it's over now and you're safe."

"No, Chad. It's not over. It's worse than you could ever guess. I lost Taffy. I tried to keep her, but—"

"I know. You told me. But she can't be far. We'll find her." He mounted his horse and reached out a hand to pull her up. "Let's go."

"You don't understand!" Andi insisted as she settled herself behind her brother. "I know where Taffy is—she's on the Livingston ranch. "But"—she swallowed and tightened her hold around Chad's waist—"she doesn't belong to me. I—I gave her to Felicity."

"You *what?*" Chad demanded. Then he softened his voice. "Maybe you'd better tell me the whole story." He urged the horse forward. "We've got a ways to go."

In a rush of words, Andi poured out the events of the past three weeks—the drifter who stole Taffy, the kindness of the Garduño family, and her futile attempts to locate Taffy in the towns they passed through. She explained how she'd come to the Lazy L and what she'd done there as a servant. She omitted nothing, not even her plan to save Felicity's horse by stealing it.

"The horse turned out to be Taffy," she said. "I guess I went sort of crazy when I saw Felicity hitting her. I—I didn't think. I just rushed in and tried to stop her." She took a deep breath and told the rest of her story in a hurry. Felicity's cruelty was not something she wanted to dwell on. "And so I signed the paper," Andi finished sorrowfully. "I had no choice—not when I heard you were all here on the Lazy L, looking for me."

"You were backed into a corner, all right," Chad agreed. "You made the right choice."

"But I lost Taffy. Can you ever forgive me for that?"

Chad brought the horse to a stop. He shifted around to look at Andi, his eyes full of compassion. "Forgiving you is the easy part, little sister. The hard part is learning to live with what's happened." He sighed. "I'm sorry about Taffy. It hurts to lose something you love, and the pain doesn't go away. But you need to know we would sacrifice Taffy in an instant to get you back. If you'd figured that out a couple of weeks ago, you could have saved yourself a lot of grief—and the rest of us, too." He turned around and urged the horse into a canter.

Andi laid her head against her brother's strong back and squeezed her eyes shut to keep the tears from flowing. Chad was right. She'd have to live with what she'd done. It was a punishment worse than any her mother could think up. Going to the barn each morning and finding an empty stall would be a continual reminder of how foolish she'd been. She didn't know if she could bear it.

But she had to. She'd made her choice.

Although Andi rode behind her brother in perfect safety, she couldn't help shuddering when she caught sight of the Lazy L ranch house. It rose before her like a bad dream when they cantered up the broad, shady lane and into the yard. She tightened her hold around Chad's waist and whispered, "Felicity told me not to come back here."

"Don't worry," he assured her. "You're with me. She can't hurt you—ever again." He slowed the horse to a trot and called out in his typical exuberant manner, "Mother! Where are you? Justin? I'm back!"

Chad pulled his horse up next to the hitching post and lowered Andi to the ground. "Where is everybody?" he called in a loud voice, dismounting and slinging the reins carelessly around the post.

The door to the Livingston home opened. Randle Livingston strode onto the veranda, followed by Andi's mother, sister, and two brothers.

"Chad!" Elizabeth exclaimed, hurrying along the brick walkway. "You're back from town already? What did you learn from the sheriff about—?"

"Mother!" Andi shouted.

"Andrea?" Her mother's voice was an astonished whisper.

Andi pushed past Chad, raced up the walkway, and threw herself into her mother's welcoming embrace. Looking up into her mother's face, she saw lines of worry and fear etched across her features. *She's all worn out because of me.* "I'm *so* sorry, Mother."

Elizabeth nodded wordlessly and held Andi close. She looked up as Chad approached. "How did you find her?"

"Apparently, she's been in a shed about five or six miles east of here." His face hardened. "Held there until she agreed to sign over Taffy to Livingston's daughter. I met up with her on the road to town.

Quite a walk for a young girl." He eyed Randle Livingston with distaste. "You've got a lot of explaining to do, mister."

An uneasy expression filled Randle's face at this news. "The girl disappeared a couple of days ago, but I thought she'd run off. I assure you, I had no idea she was still on my ranch. Had I known, I would have certainly intervened."

Chad clenched his fists and took a step toward the man. His eyes flashed. "I suppose you know nothing about my sister's whipping, either."

In the heavy silence that followed, Andi could hear the rustling of trees and the quiet swishing of a horse's tail. She felt her mother tighten her arms around her and heard the quick intake of her breath. From the corner of her eye she watched Felicity slowly lower herself onto the porch swing and clasp her fingers together in her lap. Standing beside her, Mrs. Nelson watched closely. A thoughtful frown creased her forehead.

Randle broke the silence with a deep sigh. "An unfortunate accident. I apologize." He smiled at Andi's mother. "You know how quickly these things get blown out of proportion, Mrs. Carter. It was nothing more than a misunderstanding between the girls over a horse. It's all settled now, isn't it, Felicity?"

"Indeed it is, Papa."

Randle turned back to Elizabeth. "You see? It's over. I hope you'll accept my sincere apologies and let the matter go."

Andi knew better than to interrupt her elders, but she could hardly contain herself. She wanted to leap at Mr. Livingston and make him tell the truth.

Chad saved her from doing anything so reckless. "Sure, Livingston," he offered generously. "We'll forget the whole thing. Just return my sister's horse, and we'll be on our way."

Andi's heart swelled with love for Chad. Dizzy with hope, she straightened up to listen.

"I'm afraid that will be impossible," Randle stated bluntly. He motioned to Felicity, who rose and came to stand beside her father. "My daughter has a signed bill of sale for the horse. She told me she got it the day before your sister disappeared."

That's a lie! Andi opened her mouth to voice her outrage, but her mother's firm pressure on her arm silenced her.

Randle took the soiled bill of sale from Felicity, then pulled another piece of paper from his pocket. He waved both in Chad's face. "I paid Jon March good money for the mare. Felicity offered Andrea twenty dollars. It's all right here."

Chad snatched the papers from Randle's hand and briefly scanned them. Then he passed them to Justin, who stood quietly off to one side, watching the exchange. "You're the lawyer, Justin. These look legal to you?"

Justin skimmed Felicity's document. "It *appears* to be." He glanced up at Randle, who was nodding in satisfaction. "Except for one small detail."

"What's that?" Randle snapped.

"My sister is not of age. Her signature means nothing without mine." He sighed impatiently. "As I'm sure you were already aware." He handed back the worthless papers. "The bill of sale from the livery stable isn't legitimate, either. It's for stolen property. Please, Mr. Livingston. No more games. Admit you made a mistake. We'll give you what you paid for the mare. In addition, we'll cover the cost of her board for the past three weeks."

"No, Papa!" Felicity interrupted, stamping her foot. "She's mine."

Justin ignored the outburst. "It's a fair offer. Our brand is on the horse, and you can't produce a legitimate bill of sale. That could cause you difficulties in a court of law."

Randle chewed his lip, looking thoughtful. Finally, he spoke. "I'm sorry, Felicity. The horse is not worth the trouble these folks can give me."

"You're *not* sorry!" Felicity shrieked, bursting into tears.

Randle didn't reply. He waved a ranch hand over. "Todd. Go to the barn and bring out the palomino. I've had enough of this."

"Sure thing, boss." He strode away.

Andi watched with a pounding heart. The worst was over, she was sure. Her big brother had achieved in five minutes what all her suffering and hard work had failed to accomplish during the past three weeks—getting Taffy back. She caught Justin looking at her and grinned her thanks. He winked.

"Hey, boss!" Todd emerged from the barn, shouting. "The stall's empty. The palomino's gone!"

Chapter Seventeen

END OF THE RIDE

G*one?* Icy fingers clutched at Andi's heart. She threw a startled look at Felicity and caught her smiling slyly. *She knows where Taffy is!*

Andi wanted to shake the wretched girl. Then she remembered—she'd made her choice. She'd given Taffy up so she could go home. Getting her horse back had been an unexpected miracle. Now it appeared as if Felicity would win, after all. Andi didn't know if she could lose Taffy a second time. She took a deep, shaky breath. *Help me, God,* she pleaded silently. *I can't do this alone.*

"This has gone far enough." Mrs. Nelson's voice crackled with irritation. She marched down the porch steps and planted herself in front of her employer. Her gray eyes snapped. "I'm ashamed that Felicity has been allowed to act like this. I've overlooked many of her actions in the past, out of loyalty to this family. But—*this* it's it's not decent. I won't stand for it." She drew herself up. "You may dismiss me if you like, sir, but I will be silent no longer. You must do something about your daughter's behavior—before it's too late."

"Mrs. Nelson!" Randle exclaimed. "You forget yourself."

The housekeeper set her jaw. "I will finish what I have to say. Then if you wish, I will pack my things and leave." She drew a deep breath. "Mr. Livingston, you imagine Felicity as a heartbroken little girl still mourning her mother's death. You comforted her then by giving in to her every whim. It's become a dangerous habit. I've expressed my concerns on many occasions, but you've brushed them aside like so many discarded rags." Suddenly, her determined look melted. She drew a handkerchief from her apron pocket and wiped her eyes.

Andi watched in bewilderment. Mrs. Nelson *crying*? Over *Felicity*? It was incredible.

The housekeeper sniffed back her tears. "Felicity is no longer a child. She's nearly a grown woman and has not yet learned self-control or consideration for others. I love her, Mr. Livingston, and I was afraid. She was so set on keeping that horse—to the point of acting irrationally." She stared at Randle, her eyes haunted. "The Carter girl was *locked in a shed*. What if Felicity had somehow been prevented from going out there? Andrea could have met her death. What then, sir?"

Randle paled. It was obvious his housekeeper's words were affecting him, causing him to grasp—perhaps for the first time—the enormity of his daughter's recent actions. He turned a piercing gaze on Felicity. "Where's the palomino?"

Felicity shrugged, stone-faced.

"I saw Matt leading the mare toward town, not too long after you folks arrived," Mrs. Nelson supplied, tilting her head at Elizabeth.

Randle nodded. "Then she's at the livery." He bowed slightly to Andi's mother. "I'll saddle my horse and accompany you into town. Jon will be more willing to hand over the mare if I'm along. Besides," he added, grim-faced. "I believe he and I have a little matter of a stolen horse to discuss."

"Papa!" Felicity's voice broke. "What about *me*?"

Randle turned and regarded his daughter coldly. "You have shamed me today, Felicity," he said in a voice that made Andi's eyes open wide in astonishment. "All because of your obsession over a horse. Mrs. Nelson is right. I've been blind to your faults for too long. Now my eyes are open and there will be some changes." He drew in a long, ragged breath. "I only pray for all our sakes that it is not too late."

Felicity's face went white at her father's words. She clasped her hands tightly and blinked back tears. "Papa," she whispered. "What are you saying? How can you—?"

"Enough!" There was no hint of gentleness in Randle's voice. "Go to your room. I will deal with you when I return."

Felicity fled up the walk, sobbing. With a smile and a nod of approval at Randle, Mrs. Nelson turned and followed her young mistress into the house.

"So! What are we all standing around for?" Mitch's cheerful voice jerked Andi's attention from where she stood, staring after Felicity's retreating form. He picked her up and gave her a hug. "Let's get Taffy and go home."

©

Once she was safely home again, Andi didn't care what kind of discipline she received. She welcomed the chance to show her family how much she appreciated their sacrifice. Her brothers had left the ranch in the hands of their foreman during the busiest time of the year—spring roundup—to search the countryside for her. It made her feel a little like the lost sheep in the parable Jesus told.

"This is one sheep who doesn't intend on ever getting lost again," she assured Taffy a few days later. She looked up and sighed. "And *that's* a promise, Lord. You took care of me when I acted so foolishly, and You brought me home." She threw her arms around her horse's neck and hugged her tight. Tears stung her eyes. "You even gave me Taffy back. Thank you for loving and forgiving me when I didn't deserve it."

With a grateful smile, she wiped her eyes and gently ran her hand over the healing cuts on her mare's neck. Chad had done a splendid job of tending to Taffy, and he had promised she'd be as good as new in a couple of weeks. Andi's own injuries had already faded to a minor annoyance.

"Two weeks should be just about right," Andi murmured, reaching for a brush. She'd been forbidden to ride for two weeks as part of her punishment. The other part included a list of chores a mile long. She'd be too busy to go anywhere but school for ages. "Which is fine by me, girl. We've had our fill of adventure, haven't we?"

Taffy nickered her agreement and nuzzled Andi's shoulder.

"*¿Señorita? ¿Dónde estás?*"

"I'm in here, Diego," she called to the ranch hand.

Diego made his way to Taffy's stall and leaned over the half-door. "The *señora* wishes you to come up to the house. You have visitors."

"Visitors?" Andi frowned and dropped the brush into the grooming box. "Who are they?"

Diego shook his head and shrugged. "*No sé, señorita.*"

Andi left Taffy's stall and followed Diego out of the barn. With a wave of thanks, she sprinted around the side of the ranch house and up the front porch. Who could be visiting her today?

She flung open the door, walked into the wide foyer, and gasped. The Garduño family stood beside her mother, looking uncomfortable and out of place.

"*¡Señor! ¡Señora! ¡Qué sorpresa!*—What a surprise! What are you doing here?"

"We came to let your family know where to find you," Nila explained. "But your mother told us you were already home, *gracias a Dios.*"

"Yes," José added with a smile. "My wife fussed and worried so much about leaving you on the Lazy L, I decided we could not let the *patrón* frighten us with his warnings to keep silent."

Andi grasped Nila by the hand. "I'm so glad you're here!" She looked at her mother. "This is the family I told you about, Mother. The ones who took care of me."

Elizabeth nodded. "Yes. We've been getting acquainted while we waited for you." She turned to José and Nila. "I'm grateful to you for looking after Andrea these past few weeks. She told me how you wanted to bring her home, but she wouldn't cooperate. How can we repay your kindness?"

José held up his hand. "Please, *señora*, it was our good fortune to find your daughter. She repaid us many times during her stay."

"There must be something we could do to show our gratitude."

"There is nothing," José insisted. He motioned to Nila. "The child is safe. We must be going." He paused. "I do have one question, *señora*. We are unfamiliar with this part of the valley. Do you know of any steady work nearby?"

Elizabeth answered without hesitation. "Indeed I do. There's work right here for your entire family. Luisa's getting on in years and would welcome your wife's help with the meals and housework." She smiled at José. "Our foreman can't seem to keep a full crew to cover all the jobs around here during the spring and summer. He'll find plenty of work for you and your son."

"*Gracias, señora.*" José bowed respectfully. "It would be an honor to work for you and your fine family."

Andi threw her arms around Rosa. "You get to stay! I know just where you can live. It's a little cabin a mile or so past the house. It will be so nice having a girl my age on the ranch. I'll teach you more English so you can go to school with me in the fall and—"

"*Chiquita,*" Nila interrupted. "Rosa will be *working.* She won't have much time for anything else."

"We'll see," Andi said with a grin. She turned to Joselito. "And *you*, Joselito. Maybe you'll become a cowboy, after all."

The boy beamed. "*Sí. Un vaquero.* I would like that very much."

"Mother?" Andi asked. "While you're getting everything settled, may I take Rosa and Joselito to see Taffy?"

Her mother smiled. "Of course."

Andi grinned. "She's right out back. Come on. I'll show you." She grabbed Rosa's hand and headed for the door. "When we're in the barn, you'll have to see all the stalls I've been mucking out since I got home." She made a face. "Chad saved them for me—every one." Then she laughed. "Actually, it's not such a bad job. I've had worse."

She met Rosa's look of understanding and squeezed her hand. It was *so* good to be home!